Mafietta 2: Rise Of A Female Boss

E. W. Brooks

Dedication

Anthony Brooks, you make my world turn and my heart flutter. Thank you for encouraging me to live my dreams.

I Love You!!

A House Divided

Some people get in the game to better themselves. Those are the ones who make enough money to roll into something legit and then bail. Others are in it for the 'hood credit that comes along with it. It was never about the fame for me. It was always about the bottom line and staying out of jail. Jail sentences aren't kind to families. It tests their strength and resolve.

I held Errol down the entire time he was away and I kept our name off the radar. I could not fathom why he would want to come home and pick up where he left off. If he wanted to pick up with me—it would have to be real, and it would have to be legit. I'd become well respected in our community, and I was finally able to hold my head up after the incident with Mike. No one ever found him, and I left the weight of that on the altar one Sunday morning long ago.

This was not a lifestyle I wanted for my family—and definitely not for my children. Errol had no idea that I was four months pregnant, and I had no desire to tell him now.

Our last few conversations were filled with his dreams for the family, despite the harm they could put us in. All of my work had been for nothing. I couldn't go back to that lifestyle. We had a chance to get out, and he refused to take it.

It's a good thing I'd kept my apartment, because for now, we stood—*a house divided*.

Clarke

Living somewhere for a long time doesn't make it home, and being surrounded by certain types of people doesn't mean you're like them.

***

I used these words daily to remind myself that I was better than what I'd become. This isn't what I'd planned for myself as I studied in college, walked across the stage to get my degree, or even as I walked into the Marley Grill for the first time. On one hand, I used my business acumen to triple profits for the family, but I never imagined what would be awaiting me on the flip side of this coin.

Errol will be home in two days, and I am still unsure of my next move. All I know is that nothing is more important than the little life growing inside me. Not Errol, not this money, nor this lifestyle. I just wonder if he would understand. His vision to build a stronger family haunted me at night and robbed me of peace during my waking hours. Money can't buy love or dignity, but I won't let it rob me of the two either.

I felt a hand on my shoulder. Dee was handing me a glass of champagne. Everyone around me was happy and smiling. Every boom and trail of the fireworks sent ooohs and ahhs from the frames of the smiling faces nearby.

For them, Independence Day symbolizes freedom, but for me it is anything but. Every boom reminds me of the explosion that could be my life in a couple of days.

The idea of Errol being home added to the butterflies and nausea I already have in the pit of my stomach. How he could be so foolish? We have a perfect chance to live a legitimate life—one without the crime and bullshit, and yet, he refuses. He is committed to this incredibly dangerous lifestyle.

I forced a fake smile. "Thanks for the drink, Dee." I held the glass in the air. "Cheers!"

I set the flute on the ground and hoped the wind would knock it over.

Dee said, "I know you're not gonna drink that."

"What!?" I replied.
"Clarke, just stop it. I know you're pregnant," she said. "I've been with you every day for the last four months. I have two sisters with tons of kids, and I know morning sickness when I see it."

"Dee, I'm not ready to shout it to the world yet. Keep this between us until Errol gets home. These guys don't need to know this, now."

"No worries, Clarke. You're secret is safe with me," Dee replied and walked away to join the others.

I'm glad she left. I have more time with my thoughts. I always picture picket fences and private schools when I think of my children. I never imagined a father in and out of jail. Errol could be cold enough at times to bounce our baby on his knee, kiss him on the forehead, then walk away and order a hit on someone moments later with the same lips. This isn't normal. I am living some story line from a movie. All this craziness shouldn't be my life.

How could I have ever agreed to this shit? This is not who I am.
My cousins love the idea of my marrying their supplier, but how could I face my grandmother? She would beat me with scripture and cry to me as she prayed for my soul. What will I tell our son of his father?

Maybe I should just disappear and tell Errol nothing. Nah, that's a bad idea. I don't want his wrath to ever turn on me.

I was a million miles away from the crowd, and my head was spinning. The sound of a ringing phone sent me crashing back to earth. My burner phone's screen was blinking. It was Errol.

Errol

It breaks my heart to see the woman Clarke has become on my account. The soft smile that often filled her face is gone and has been replaced with worry lines. I know it is all my fault. The innocence I loved about her is gone. I never intended her to have blood on her hands. Those were my tribulations. I never wanted them to become her reality.

Most men keep their women as far away from this life as possible, but Clarke made me so damned comfortable around her. I trusted her with way too much. I don't worry that she'll ever snitch on me, and that was a bonus, but I was never prepared for the toll it would take on her.

Money, clothes, nice cars, and homes are no prize in comparison to the nights of lost sleep or the look in someone's eyes just before I pulled the trigger ending their lives. This is the thing that haunts me. This is the thing that keeps me from enjoying my Egyptian cotton sheets and makes me look over my shoulder when I drive my new BMW down the street.

Clarke was distressed, and I wish I could erase that pain. I thought the joy of having our child would save her from those feelings, but it only intensified them. She still hasn't told me about the baby, but the streets talk, even in here. She is on me more and more to leave this life, and I know that's why, but she doesn't understand—I am a KING.

I can't turn in my two-week notice and leave the company. This is not the corporate world she was used to. I pledged my life and allegiance when I became a King, and my losing my life is the only thing that would allow me to leave this world. This was life in and life out.

At the same time, I cannot allow her to leave me. It took me years to meet her again. I had no idea that I'd ever fall so deeply for her. This feeling was a long time coming, and I want to keep it.

On the other hand, she knows too much to be away from me. I am sure that her leaving me would raise eyebrows with the other Kings. They were pleasantly surprised with the way Clarke held me down when I was locked up. She gained their trust and respect, and neither came easily.

I know they won't just allow her to walk away. It is a good thing that I love Clarke because we are bound together now. There is no turning back. We will make it. We have no choice.

Besides, in two days, I'm outta this joint.

Clarke

Today is the day. I should be happy, but for some reason, I have the worst headache. I haven't felt well since dinner last night. I usually cook or have something sent from the restaurant, but I was too tired to move yesterday.

Luckily enough, Dee was here to make dinner. I was feeling a bit woozy, and she offered to stay over and keep an eye on me. As much as I hate to admit it, I was glad to have her around. Her being here meant my thoughts would be limited to the pointless bounds of our conversation instead of my overwhelming reality.

Business was booming, and we'd reached a place where it basically took care of itself, so other than making her weekly drops and reports—we'd chosen to permanently limit talk of the trade.

The last thing I remembered from last night was Dee saying something about things coming full circle, but I was so groggy. I wasn't able to make sense of it all. I do know that she helped me to bed, though. Now I was waking to the sound of my alarm. I felt sick to my stomach as my feet touched the floor, and I attempted to stand up, but I couldn't give in to today's bout of morning sickness. I had too much to do.

I was happy to see an ironed pair of slacks and button-up shirt hanging on the back of the bathroom door. Dee was on point. I knew there was a reason I keep her around. I rushed to take a shower and get ready. I had about an hour before I was scheduled to pick Errol up from the courthouse.

Eric had finally gotten Errol a bail hearing, and he reassured me that my man would be coming home today. It was a blessing that Admiral sent their cousin Baris to work with Eric and handle the legal aspect of things, so other than taking care of Errol's day to day, I'd been able to keep my hands clean and my name away from that part of the business. Eric advised me against picking Errol up, but I insisted. It had been months since I'd been able to touch him, and despite the issues that surrounded us, I couldn't wait any longer.

A steady stream of water showered down onto my face and trickled down my neck to the rest of my body. I felt the weight of the last few months wash away from me and run to its escape down the drain.

When Errol gets here, I can go back to just being me.

I rushed into my clothes and found Dee sitting on my bed, waiting.

"Hey Clarke, do you need me to tighten up your hair real quick? I know you don't have time for a full breakfast, but I toasted you a bagel and made you a cup of decaf to grab on your way out of the door." I smiled and breathed a sigh of relief. "Thanks, Dee. You've been a lifesaver."

Dee quickly pulled my hair into the perfect high ponytail, and I was finally ready to go. I took a quick bite of the bagel and grabbed the coffee cup. As I took my first sip, Dee said, "Clarke, I have been waiting for months and still no Mike. Do you have any idea what could have happened to him?"

"He left our last meeting pretty upset with me, but I haven't seen him since," I replied.

Dee stared straight into my soul and asked, "You don't think the Kings did anything to him, do you?"

I swallowed the wrong way, and coffee spewed from my mouth as I began to cough. Dee's face was filled with a look I'd never seen before. She seemed perplexed, but angered. Just then, I knew Dee had become suspicious of me.

She quickly composed herself, took a look at her

watch, and said, "Clarke, you'd better get going if you're gonna get Errol on time."

Dee locked up for me and followed me down the steps to the parking lot. "What the hell?" I screamed. Three of my tires were flat. Immediately, my heart began to race, and I felt a sharp pain in my stomach. Vomit began to spurt from my mouth, and my blouse was ruined.

What was I going to do? I had to pick Errol up in less than half an hour, and I had no time to change. My legs were beginning to feel like jelly beneath me. Beads of sweat formed on my forehead, and I knew there was no way I would make it to the courthouse.

"Dee, I don't know what's happening. I need you to run and grab Errol for me. We were supposed to go to the house, but bring him here. That will give me some time to get myself together. Have Rocko come by and take care of the car."

"No problem, Clarke. It's a good thing I was here. Get some rest, and I'll take care of everything."

"Thanks, Dee, you're a lifesaver. Just get my baby home to me." She gave me an uncomfortable smirk as she got into her car and drove away. Oh hell! Dee knew. I'd been avoiding the subject for months, but it was obvious that the time to deal with the issue was fast approaching.

I felt like shit. My knees were weak, and my stomach was killing me. I was in no shape to greet Errol when he arrived. I rushed to the medicine cabinet on wobbly legs. I scarfed down two Tylenol and a Phenergan. Then I grabbed my cell phone and headed to bed.

The room started to spin as I dialed Rocko's number. He quickly answered, "Hey, cuz, what's up?"

"I don't have time to explain. Come right now. It's important."

He responded, "I got you, cuz. I'm on my way."

I ended the call just as the room began to spin. I couldn't keep my eyes open any longer. I'd lost my fight with the sandman and fell off into a deep slumber.

I woke as the alarm system announced that someone was entering the front door. I hoped it wasn't Errol. My shirt was still covered with vomit, and my hair was a mess. I struggled to sit up in the bed as Rocko walked through the bedroom door.

"Cuz, what are you doing home? I thought you were

picking up Errol today."

"That was the plan, but I woke up to an upset stomach and three flat tires. My clothes were ruined, and I was running late so I sent Dee instead."

"Why didn't you call me, cuz?"

"I wasn't thinking. She was here and offered to go."

"Girl, your man has been in jail for months, and you send another woman to pick him up? What is wrong with you? That was a bad move, cuz."

"Well. hit me when I'm down, Rocko."

He laughed. "I'm just saying."

"Hell, you're right. Send Arvin to the courthouse. I'll call Dee," I responded.

I used my speed dial to call Dee, but heard a vibration coming from my bathroom.

Rocko looked at me and rushed to meet the sound. He came back with Dee's phone in hand. "Call Arvin to see what's going on. Wake me up when you find out," I said.

Dee is really getting beside herself. First the question about Mike and now this. I liked Dee because she was methodical and loyal. Her cell was always attached to her hand or her hip. She never left it anywhere.

I have to keep a close eye on her from now on. Thoughts of finally squaring off with Dee filled my head as I drifted off to sleep.

I am not sure how much time passed, but I woke with a start as the alarm announced that the front door was opening. I sat up in bed, to find a line of saliva extending from my mouth to the pillow. Man, that must have been some good sleep, because I didn't feel the puddle of moisture I'd been lying in.

Oh, shit! Errol was here! I couldn't let him see me like this. I ignored the feeling of nausea of that overwhelmed me as I jumped into the shower. I hadn't seen my man in months, and our first encounter would not consist of a vomit-covered shirt and disheveled hair.

The immediate feeling of sickness began to subside as the warm water pelted my face. I watched the water flow over my increasingly large breasts and down to my protruding stomach. For now, I looked like I simply gained a few pounds. I had no idea how or if I should hide this from Errol, but from the look of things, I wouldn't have long to decide.

Muscle memory took over as I rushed to wash my body and jump into a robe. I searched for the shea-butter-enriched lotion that would hopefully reduce the likelihood of any pregnancy-related stretch marks. I found a seat on the purple bench in the bathroom as I applied lotion to the underside of my belly and rest of my body. I pulled my hair into a high ponytail and was just standing to walk from the bathroom into the bedroom when I heard a knock.

My heart fluttered, and butterflies filled my stomach as I said, "Come in!" The next couple of seconds felt like an eternity. What should I do? Should I stand up, sit down, lie on the bed, or simply open my robe, place my hands on my hips and see if he would figure out that we had a little one on the way.

I chose the latter and was beginning to pull the tie to open my robe when I heard Rocko's voice. "Put your clothes back on, nasty, it's just me." A gut-wrenching laugh filled the room as we both considered what had just happened.

"What do you want, Rocko? I thought you were Errol."

"Uh, cuz, that was obvious, but some cat named Hiram just got here talking about Mandell sent him here to wait on Errol."

An immediate sense of dread and uneasiness filled my body as I considered all of the reasons Mandell, the Kings' supplier, would send his own watchdog. This nigga was not about to ruin the homecoming I'd played time and time again in my head.

I couldn't just be Clarke today as I planned. It wasn't even noon, and I was already being forced into my alter ego.

Hiram Comes

This unfamiliar figure turned as he heard the heels of my Tom Ford stilettos hit the linoleum tile behind him. As he finally faced me, I extended my hand. "Hello, Hiram, I am Clarke. I don't believe we've met, but more important, what brings you to our neck of the woods?"

My face depicted a woman—cool, calm, and collected. However, in my head, I was thinking, "What the fuck!" This dude sounded Jamaican, but he was white! This had to be some bullshit. Who was this guy? Mandell would never send a white guy to do business, would he?

I had to work through this critically. He was well dressed, well groomed, and he was wearing that identifying ring. Oh, hell. He was really with the Kings.

"Well, I have come to see how Errol, the man with whom we share mutual interest and admiration, is faring now that he is back at home," he replied.

This man was a hard read. He didn't crack a smile. His hands were palm up on his lap, so he didn't appear to be hiding anything, but something about this guy just didn't sit right with me.

"While I'm glad you are here, I do wish you would have waited until after his homecoming to make yourself known—Hiram, right?"

"I can certainly understand your concern, Clarke, but that isn't the way things are done in our business. Being a King doesn't always afford one the privacy they may like."

"Maybe, but don't those who serve Kings serve at their pleasure? I think everyone here would be pleased if you were to come back a bit later. I haven't seen Errol in months, and our first moments aren't ones that I care to share. I am sure you can understand. Rocko, please hand Hiram his hat."

I turned my attention back to the stranger at my counter. "Please join us for dinner this evening at Errol's. That will be a more fitting meeting place. Please let Mandell know that we do appreciate his concern. However, this conversation is better had later this evening."

Hiram was apparently aggravated but remained a gentleman and made his way to the door, which Rocko was holding open.

"Oh, Hiram. We love dessert wine. A nice moscato would be nice. Does six o'clock work for you?"

"I will see you there. Until then, please give Errol my regards." Hiram slowly placed his hat on the top of his head, winked, and was gone.

"Rocko, get Admiral on the phone, right now. Then call and get some troops here."

Daddy Is Home

I was so engrossed in damage control that I didn't hear the alarm announce the opening door as Errol entered for the first time in months. We'd spent most of our time at his house before he went away, but I wanted to keep our reunion quaint and quiet, and my apartment was the best place for that.

I couldn't hear past the whistle of the kettle as I boiled water to make tea. I rushed to remove it from the flame when I felt the touch of familiar arms wrapping themselves around me. There was no need to turn around. My King was home.

For the first time in months, I was able to give way to the vulnerability nestled deep inside the new woman I'd become. Finally, I could relax and go back to being a normal woman having a baby and planning a wedding. The rest of the stresses would revert to Errol. Things would finally be as they had been. His embrace reassured me of that.

Suddenly, my spirit was flooded with conflicting emotions. I loved Errol and was glad he was home, but he had to get out of the game. I wanted to tell him about our little one, the legal investments; but on the other hand, I wanted to cry for the woman I am. I'd lost something since he'd been away, and I needed him to know it. I didn't sign up to become an assassin or Mafietta, as I was so frequently called, but in this moment words escaped me.

I turned to meet the widest smile and brightest eyes. Immediately I could feel he was equally glad to see me. He moved his arms up to cradle my face and kissed me so passionately that the love behind it resonated down to my toes. This is what love felt like, and I was not giving it up. I need to be loved, and Errol loved me. Love would just have to conquer the rest.

That was the only thing keeping me from slapping the shit out of him right now. Errol's kiss knocked me off my feet. His warm lips against mine made me feel gravity was suspended. Space and time in this moment only existed for us. The energy and connection between him and me stopped the world.

Suddenly Mike, Hiram, the Kings, the business— nothing mattered. The love I felt in this moment could surpass and overcome it all. We were connected, and I wouldn't allow the world to separate us. My heart fluttered, and my legs were wobbly. I am not sure when we disconnected, or when I passed out, but I woke up in the middle of the kitchen floor, wrapped in the arms of my fiancé.

Rocko was bringing over a cold compress. He handed it to Errol and in one swift movement, he lifted me in his strong arms and carried me up the stairs to the bedroom. I tried to open my mouth to speak, but my head was spinning. While I searched my brain for words, I felt a finger fall against my lips. Errol said, "Baby, I missed you, too. Don't talk now. Just relax. There will be plenty of time for words."

He carried me all the way to my bedroom and laid me gently on the bed. Suddenly, the weeks of stress were upon me at once, and I was exhausted. I struggled to keep my eyes open as Errol began to unbutton my blouse. In another swift movement, he unbuckled my bra, and his hands began to trace my breasts.

My eyes opened long enough to see the gargantuan smile on his face. Then the sandbags returned, and my efforts to hold open my eyes were for naught. I was asleep again. Exhaustion consumed me, despite my will to be ever present in the moment.

I woke to a start as I felt Errol's hand leave my stomach. The bed shook a bit as he balanced himself on his knees above me. His smile was replaced with a look of concern. "Clarke, your stomach; does this mean what I think it means? Are you giving me a child?"

Those words penetrated my grogginess. Again, my mouth opened but offered no voice to the silence permeating the room. A streak of warmth ran down both sides of my face, but they were quickly replaced with soft hands that brushed the tears away as I shook my head up and down.

Errol jumped to his feet. The room was filled with sound as he pumped his fist to the sky, screaming, "YES, YES!!"

I felt strengthened by his reaction and was surprisingly able to prop myself up on the pillows behind me.

My weak voice responded, "You're happy about this?"

"Absolutely, my love. Why wouldn't I be?"

"I was just thinking that with everything going on, maybe having a baby right now isn't something you wanted to do. I thought maybe you'd leave; say you didn't have time for this or that I'd trapped you."

"Clarke, why would you think a foolish thing like

that? This thing we have between us is forever."

The words pierced my spirit like a sword. I knew he was excited about our baby, but I also knew I'd never be able to leave him.

"Errol, who is Hiram?" I asked. The face of a happy expectant father was suddenly replaced by a look I didn't recognize. I saw rage, anger, and a man I didn't know.

"How do you know Hiram?" he asked, trying to remain calm.

"He came by here today to wait for you. Baby, didn't you know he was coming?"

For the first time since his return, Errol had no words for me, only a look of utter astonishment, so I continued. "I asked him to leave so that you and I could have a proper reunion. He didn't seem too thrilled about my request, but he conceded after I invited him to dinner at your place tonight." I said.

"You did what?" Errol retorted.

"Hell, what did you want me to do? I had to get him outta here. I never disclosed my address to your people. How does he know I live here, Errol?"

Strength found me as I stood up and walked over to Errol. "How the hell does he know where I live?" I shouted. "Tell me! Tell me, damn it!"

Errol's legs turned to spaghetti as he collapsed onto the bench at the foot of my bed. He wasn't even this shaken up in New Orleans. I'd never seen him this way. I was pissed all over again. "I envisioned a normal life. Despite everything in front of me, I envisioned a normal life; but that won't happen for me, will it?" Tears streamed down my face as I looked over to see Errol, shaking his head from side to side; face in hands. "Say it, Errol, just say it! Tell me the sentence I've accepted by being with you?" I screamed.

Errol still sat, face covered, too hurt and ashamed to look me in the face.

"Look at me, damn it! Look at me! Do you know what they call me around here, Errol? They call me Mafietta; not because it's a term of endearment—but because I had to become a killer to run this shit for you."

My body shook, and snot ran down my face. "I have blood on my hands, Errol. Blood! All for you—to protect this bullshit you've built."

I jabbed my pointer finger into his forehead as I continued to yell, "You fix this shit, and you fix it now. I refuse to bring a child into this Shotta bullshit you call a life."

He jumped up from the seat and was now in my face. "What you want me to do, Clarke—retire, just walk away? These are not the type of people you can just walk away from. Do you know how much money you made for them while I was gone? Do you think they will just let you leave? Clarke, this shit is for life. Once you become a King; you live a King and die a King. There is nothing in between. You, my dear, have become a King," he replied with a quaver in his voice. "There is no way out of this, Clarke. We are who we are, and there is no turning back. Excuse me for a minute. I need to call Hiram and the Kings."

He planted a defeated kiss on my forehead, and I was left alone. I ran to the railing and called downstairs for Rocko.

Sorry, Dee

I was wearing a brand-new Michael Kors knit dress that accentuated every curve, as I pulled up to the courthouse. I hoped that picking Errol up would allow me to stir up some shit between him and Clarke. Errol needed to know the things going on while he was away. Mike and Errol were so close before Errol got arrested. There is no way he would've ordered his death.

This bitch is getting out of control, and she has to be stopped. I knew she would try to cut me out of the business now that Errol was back, but I couldn't let that happen. Making this kind of money is addictive. Once you've gotten used to living in on $20–$30,000 a week, there is no nine-to-five job that can ever make you whole.

I couldn't wait to tell Errol about the thousands of dollars I'd spent on a private detective in search of Mike. If he knew that the detective only found one dead end and after another, maybe he would help. I needed some kind of justice. An average person could contact their local police department, but in our business, the police station was the last place I'd better be seen.

I was almost sure that Clarke was catching on to my suspicions. I blamed myself for having such a loose lip this morning. I didn't care that she knew that I'd found her out, but I couldn't afford this to happen until after I had all my ducks in a row.

Clarke was like Teflon. She worked for the best criminal attorney in town, and with his influence, no one would believe me. I had to take matters into my own hands. I thought flattening her tires and slipping her an Ambien would give me time to get to Errol, but the bitch outsmarted me.

By the time I got there, Errol and Arvin were laughing as they walked down the courthouse steps. I knew there was no need for me. I would've looked like a fool walking up to Errol saying I came to take you home, and Clarke knew that, too.

I reached for my cell phone. Then I realized I'd left it on the counter in Clarke's bathroom, but she wasn't the only one that could carry a burner phone. It was time that I got my own.

Zap Zip Cellular was running a two for one special. Maybe the stars were starting to align for me.

***

I walked out of the store with a bag full of technology. I was looking down to grab my keys from my purse. My bags began to rattle as I walked straight into someone. I looked up to see who I'd bumped into, and there was Black.

"What up, Dee? Did Clarke send you here for another burner?" He chuckled. "You know Mafietta don't trust nobody."

I was startled, but I had to play along. "Yeah, man, you know Clarke, but I left my phone at her place, and I have to get back. See you at the party tonight," I said.

My hands shook as I tried to press the button on my keyless entry fob. The key fell to the ground.

"Girl, you better get yourself together. No room for that shit in what we do. Holla at you later."

He jumped into his tricked-out Camaro and was finally out of my hair. I threw the bag in the trunk and was off to Clarke's to grab my real phone.

So Glad I Can Add

Rocko said, "Clarke, you're crazy. There is no way you can get a new place, and these niggas not know it."

"Yes, hell, I can and I will. Call Grandma, send her some money, and have her put it in her name. I need a place to crash, just in case shit here gets too real."

"You're the boss, cuzzo."

"Oh, and Rocko, keep this between you, me, and Jesus. Errol can't know."

Just then, the door swung open, and Errol said, "Errol can't know what?"

Rocko responded, "If she tells you; it won't be a surprise, man." Then my cousin turned to me and kept talking. "Aight, cuz; I gotta get outta here to get ready for the party, but I'm on it. Arvin and Lil' Stupid are outside."

I closed my bedroom door, ready to have some alone time with Errol. He questioned me before I could turn around. "Babe, did you make all of the bank deposits for the Kings?"

"Hell, nawl," I responded. "There was no way I was going to touch that shit. I know how you people are about your money. Why, what's up?"

"The Kings are short just over half a million dollars, and they're wondering if you're responsible."

"Uh, not me. I am not that girl. Scott handled all of that, but your wifey is no fool. Check the bottom drawer right there in the nightstand. There is a ledger in there that reflects every deposit made to every account as well as the money that was given to Scott to forward to the Kings."

"You know he'll never admit to this, right?" Errol said.

"He doesn't have to. He's been sending me weekly spreadsheets since you left. I'll print you a copy, and you can check that against the payments the Kings received. Is that why Hiram is here?"

"Yes, babe."

"Well, what did he come to do?" I asked. "Did he come for me?"

"No, he came to ask a question, but understand—the Kings only ask once, and you better be right when you answer," he said.

"How are you going to expose Scott?" I asked.

"Clarke, I got this. I know you're tired of being Mafietta. Trust me. I got this one. Tonight, you just focus on being beautiful. I'll handle the rest. I'm going to take Scott and Black with me to sort this thing out. Arvin is downstairs, but where is Dee?" Errol inquired.

"Something is up with her. She is starting to ask questions about Mike. Although she has never told me directly, I've heard that she even hired a private detective. I didn't want to dump all of this on you right now, but I really feel Dee is going to be a problem. She chased me in my dreams for about half an hour today, and we both know my dreams don't lie."

Errol chuckled, "Clarke, don't tell me you really thought she wouldn't find you out. Are you really that naïve?"

"Yes!" I returned. "I was never prepared to deal with Dee and definitely not the issue of Mike, but she knows, baby. My plan was to pick you up myself, but I woke up to three flat tires, and then I got sick. Coffee is usually the one thing that soothes me, but today was the total opposite. I was sick. I mean, the throwing-up-all-over-my-clothes sick. Then she left her phone here. Dee never leaves her phone anywhere. We're gonna have to deal with her, Errol. She knows too much."

"You're probably right, but for now just keep her close. We'll deal with this shit once Hiram leaves. We have enough on our plate for now. I feel like I've taken care of everyone today except you, but don't worry. When the lights go out tonight, it's all about you, babe."

My baby's daddy kissed me and my growing stomach good-bye, and again, I was alone. I rushed to the closet, grabbed my pink nine millimeter with the Swarovski crystal grip, checked the safety, and placed it under my pillow.

I locked my bedroom door and lay down for a nap. I had about four hours before the party, and I needed them all to prepare.

The Party

"What the fuck, Admiral?" Errol screamed into the receiver.

"Man, you know the game. You know the protocol. Shit looks crazy when you have a woman take over, and suddenly the drops are short. It was bad enough that you left a woman to run your affairs in the first place. Do you know what kind of smoothing it took for the Kings to accept her? And now the money is messed up. We've killed for less, Errol."

"I am my own enforcer, Admiral. I've never needed help from the Kings to handle my business, and I don't need them to figure things out for me now."

"Well, lil' bro, I hope you've figured this thing out because if not, Hiram is locked and loaded."

"What the fuck is wrong with him? How dare he threaten the woman I love?" Errol screamed. "If he's gonna point the gun at anyone, it had better be Scott."

"Scott?" Admiral replied, confused. "Why would Scott do a thing like that?"

"You'll have to ask him. Check your e-mail. I just sent you Scott's financials. His reports to Clarke show no error. Check them against your receipts and get back to me. In the meantime, tell Hiram to fall back."

"You got it, lil' bro, but you better be right."

"Admiral, there are two things Clarke knows—that's money and the law. Just have a look and hit me back." With that, Errol ended the call and called his Realtor.

"Cathy, is everything in order?"

"Absolutely, Errol. Everything was completed according to the boards you sent over," the woman on the other end of the phone replied.

"Great, see you tonight. And Cathy, make sure you keep this one under the radar."

"You got it, Errol. See you later!"

"Scooooott!" Errol called.

Within seconds, Scott appeared. "What's up, man?"

"I wanna get up to speed with the cash accounts. Grab your reports for me and let's chop it up."

"Errol, you are just getting home. Don't worry yourself with that now. Focus on that extravagant-ass party you're having tonight," Scott replied nervously.

"If I'm back. I have to be all the way back. Grab the

files. I'll meet you in my office in ten. I need to make another call."

Scott walked away, head down and defeated. Errol made one more call to Admiral.

The phone only rang once, and the brothers were connected again. "Admiral, send me the receipts as you have them. I want to take a look myself."

"No need. I checked it out, and the cart stops with Scott. His mainland reports don't match the ones sent here."

"Damn!" Errol screamed as his fist pounded the table. "He, of all people, knows what happens when money disappears. What a way to come home. Bring Hiram up to speed, and we'll deal with this shit after the party. No need in making a good evening worse."

**

Scott sat in front of Errol's merlot cherry-finished Oxmoor desk staring into the glass door on the hutch behind the oversize and intimidating wingback swivel chair that demanded the respect of those sitting opposite.

Errol walked across the spacious office, past the gun-filled cherry credenza, to the daunting chair behind the massive desk.

"Did you grab those reports?" Errol asked.

Shaky hands passed the reports over to Errol.

Errol said, "Scott, you're right. This isn't the time for business. I am just home, and there is the party of all parties going on tonight. We'll deal with this later."

Scott's demeanor changed completely. He no longer cowered in the face of the oversize chair and the King sitting in it. His head was lifted, and his chest stuck out as a man again. Errol noticed the countenance change but spoke nothing of it.

It broke his heart to see money end a thirty-year friendship, but money had a way of revealing one's true heart and intentions. Damned shame that Scott didn't measure up after all this time. There was no time to mope; besides, Errol had learned to live with regret.

"Go home and lively up yourself. I'll see you at the spot for the party. You have the address, right?"

"Sure thing, man. Check you out at eight."

Scott rose and said, "Errol, I'm glad you're back.

Mafietta could be a real bitch." He smiled and walked away.

Errol remained calm, despite the bull raging inside him. He fought the urge to grab the machete, sheathed on the underside of his desk.

Scott had no idea he was getting away by the skin of his teeth. However, the fool didn't know when enough was enough. He turned again to ask, "Hey, Errol, do you have any idea why Hiram is here?"

"I assumed to share in the joy of my homecoming," Errol responded.

"I don't know, man," Scott replied cockily, "he's always been quick to check a bitch."

As he opened his mouth to formulate his next sentence, the machete flew across the room. It landed in Scott's chest so deeply, his right lung collapsed.

Errol walked over to the credenza, grabbed a Glock, and stood over his old friend as he coughed, choking on his own blood.

"Why'd you do it, man?" Errol asked.

"You know why, man," Scott replied between coughing up globs of blood that stained his shirt and the carpet. You chose a woman over me! You chose a bitch…"

Scott fell silent and after the bang, Errol looked down to see his lifelong friend shot in the head.

A tear fell from Errol's face to the floor and it was done. That was all the time he had to mourn the disloyal.

He went back to his desk to call Admiral.

"Yo, call Hiram to come clean this shit up."

"Errol, you didn't?" asked a concerned Admiral.

"I had to, Kings don't tolerate disrespect."

"I'll make the call. Now, do me a favor King Shotta. Put the guns away, and enjoy the rest of your evening."

Errol hung up the phone, walked past his friend for the last time, and closed the door.

Black stood yards away from the door, eyes filled with tears, afraid to fall.

"He was a thief," Errol said as he walked past one of the last hometown friends he had left. "He was a thief."

Black walked behind his friend and leader and watched as he collapsed into the raised chair at the kitchen counter.

"You should never have to dead a friend over money. Never! He did it to frame Clarke. He admitted the shit to me, man. He admitted it."

Black had no idea what to say. He knew the code, but his heart broke, just as Errol's did for his dead friend. He walked over to a cabinet on the far side of the room and returned with two crystal glasses and a bottle of Jamaican rum.

Then two friends had a drink to remember the dead.

***

Clarke woke feeling rested. She yawned and stretched as she rolled over to look at the time. Wow, it was already five o'clock. She had less than two hours to get dressed and go to the house in Churchill Downs where they were hosting the party. The homes there were amazing. The community was gated, and the average family income was just shy of a million dollars.

It was a community where people minded their business. Maybe that's why Errol chose it. Clarke began to feel a bit nauseated as she stood to get out of bed. She immediately reached for the soda crackers on the nightstand beside her bed. After eating a couple and taking a sip of ginger ale, she was able to keep moving.

She walked over to her closet to get her dress, an A-line, tent style created by one of the Port City's best designers. Stephen Holland designed clothes that made Clarke look chic and not pregnant. He'd also picked out a pair of stylish wedges and the most perfect accessories.

Clarke was excited to see her man again. In days past, she would've worn something a bit more contemporary to meet the man she had not seen in months, but Errol would understand. Her head was still spinning from their previous conversation. While she hated to let loose on him like that, it felt good to get those emotions off her chest. For the first time in a very long time, Clarke was happy.

She decided to run downstairs and grab an apple. Being pregnant and hungry was the worst. She hit the stereo's on button as she unlocked the door to make her trek to the kitchen. Just as she began to close her eyes and sing along, her foot caught something. She struggled to keep her balance.

She opened her eyes to find Dee sitting at the top of her stairs. "What are you doing sitting up here like that?" Clarke asked in an aggravated tone. "Why didn't you knock on the door?"

"Arvin told me you were asleep, but I ran up here to grab my phone. I left it this morning. I couldn't get it, though. Your door was locked. Since when do you lock your doors to sleep, Clarke?"

"Since now, Dee. I'm starting to dream some real crazy shit, and you know my dreams don't lie. I'm hoping it's the baby and my hormones. I'd hate to lay out someone I trust."

Dee's eyes got big for second, but she quickly regained control of her reaction. "Hey, Clarke, do you mind if I run in your room and grab my phone?"

"If you'll run downstairs and grab me an apple, I'll get it for you," Clarke responded slyly.

Dee walked away, perplexed. Something about Clarke was changing, and she needed to get to the bottom of things before she came up missing, too.

When Dee returned with the apple, she found her phone lying on the bed.

Clarke was in the bathroom and called out, "Dee, I

know you need to get ready, too. Arvin is here to drive me, so I'll just meet you there."

"Don't you need me to do your hair?" Dee asked.

"Nah, babe, I have it covered. Thanks anyway. Girl, stop worrying about me. Go home, take care of you, and I'll meet you there in a bit."

While Clarke was being as nice as she always had, Dee felt something was amiss. Her suspicions were confirmed as she met Tina at the door.

"Tina, what are you doing here?"

"Ms. Clarke asked me to come do her hair and makeup for the party."

"Why would she call you?"

"I don't know, Ms. Dee, but when Ms. Clarke calls, you have to answer."

"I guess you're right, Tina. See you at the party."

"Okay, Ms. Dee."

"Oh, and Tina, Clarke is not quite herself today. Let me know if anything strange happens."

Tina didn't turn around to respond.

***

"Hey, Ms. Clarke. Is Ms. Dee okay? She seemed a little pissed that you asked me to do your hair."

"That's her problem now, isn't it?" Dee asked as she tied her robe.

"I know, Ms. Clarke, but I just don't want her mad at me."

"She isn't the one you need to be worried about. What else did she say?"

"Um, nothing much. She told me to keep an eye out on you, because you are not quite yourself today. She just wants me to let her know if anything strange happens."

"Tina, has Dee been acting strange to you?"

"Maybe a little. She's really become obsessed with figuring out what happened to her boyfriend, and it seems that the private detective she hired can't come up with any answers."

"Tina, how do you feel about taking a more active role in the organization?"

"Oh, Ms. Clarke, I'd love to."

"Great. For now you'll be my personal assistant, but let's not tell Dee yet. I don't want to put anything else on her. She's stressed out enough."

"No worries, Ms. Clarke. I gotcha."

"Oh, and Tina, stop calling me Ms. I am not that much older than you, and if I am, you'll never know it."

***

Dee was blindingly furious. It was undeniable that Clarke knew something was up. Thoughts rushed through Dee's mind faster than she could process them. She was coming undone. She pulled into the liquor store on Sixteenth Street, grabbed a bottle of Hennessey, and headed home. She needed something to quiet her mind.

Dee didn't even turn on the lights as she walked to the kitchen cabinet and grabbed a glass and a small tin box. She poured herself a healthy glass of the dark brown liquor, took two large gulps, and pulled a prerolled joint from the small box. She grabbed the remote to turn on the stereo.

The apartment was so quiet she heard the burn of the paper as she lit her medication. She took one deep puff, and smoke filled her head. She instantly began to feel better. The voices weren't as loud. She gulped even more of her Hennessey. She needed all the courage she could get.

Her trance was broken as Freddie Jackson's "All I'll Ever Ask of You" came through her speakers. Teardrops turned into a flood, and hurt turned into anger. Someone had to pay. There was no doubt that Clarke was one of the last people to see Mike alive, even though no one would confirm it.

Now she got to prance around carrying a baby she didn't even know she wanted to keep. She and Errol would look at each other and smile all night or exchange playful glances and passionate kisses, while I have nothing and no one to hold on to.

Dee poured another drink and threw it all back at once. Her walk was a bit unsteady, but her mission was clear. Tonight she would confront the mighty King and if necessary, bring the kingdom to his knees.

She turned on the shower and went into the bedroom to grab her robe. She reentered the hazy bathroom and almost tripped as she lifted her leg to step into the tub. As the water hit her face and steam entered her nostrils, she was reminded of her last time in the shower with Mike. For a moment, she could almost feel his hands on her body. She could see his smiling face and the wink that always fixed whatever wrongs he'd done.

The tears were back, but they were short-lived. Dee was convinced Mike had wiped them away. As she rubbed the lathered soap all over her body, she could feel his presence. She could feel him reaching for her. Dee finished her shower but continued to stand in the stream of warm running water. Her memories were enough to keep her there forever. It was only when the water turned cold that she was sent flying back to reality.

Dee stepped into her robe and inhaled. It was crazy, but she still sprayed Mike's cologne on the collar of her robe just so she'd never forget him. She grabbed a bottle of lotion and walked into the living room, where she had another drink and smoked another joint before finally dressing and leaving for the party.

It was already seven fifteen. The party started at eight, and that would give her about fifteen minutes to spare. As Drake's latest album filled the car, Dee noticed the blue lights. A sense of dread filled her body, and she quickly sobered up. She pulled to the shoulder, and a plainclothes officer emerged from an unmarked vehicle.

"Ma'am, do you know why I pulled you over?" the officer asked.

"No, sir, I don't."

"Well, you've been swerving for the last half a mile."

"Officer, that is simply not true. There is no way you would have let me be a public nuisance for that long," Dee retorted.

"Deshaunda Teal, you may be right, but don't worry. This is your lucky night. I hear you've been trying to find out what happened to your boyfriend for about four or five months now."

"How do you know my name, and why are you acting like you give a fuck about my missing boyfriend?"

"We know everything, Ms. Teal. We even know something you don't know."

"And what might that be, Officer?"

"We know that gangster lady—What's her name?—killed your boo."

A look of confirmed astonishment covered Dee's face. At that moment that Officer Vincent Rouche knew he had a mole.

"I'll tell you what, Ms. Teal, if you agree to work with us, we will get that gangster bitch who killed your man and give you immunity in the case. Oh, and we'll overlook this drunk driving. You don't have to give me an answer now. I'll just leave you with my card."

"I don't mind responding now, sir. I'll be glad to help you."

Dee extended the officer her hand and said, "If you don't mind, I have a party to attend."

A smile covered Officer Rouche's face as he walked away. He knew he had the inside connection he needed. He returned to his car and leaned over to the quiet gentleman sitting next to him. "Keep an eye on her. You know those people—they kill first and ask questions later."

"Whatever you say, boss," Dee replied.

***

Errol stepped out of the shower feeling energized and refreshed. There was nothing like being home, especially after being in the joint for almost four months. Clarke had a martini microstripe Dolce and Gabbana three-piece suit tailored and sent over with a pair of Palermo brushed-leather lace-ups for tonight's festivities.

Being with Clarke taught him to appreciate nice things. This was a $2,000 outfit, but appearances were important. The Kings in attendance, as well our business partners, need to know I am back. The new me has run even farther from the nappy-headed barefoot boy I try to forget.

Clarke walked in as he tied his shoes. She was radiant. Her tray showed enough cleavage to keep him staring all night, but not enough to interest anyone else, and her legs looked great. Errol couldn't wait to have her wrap them around him later. He'd been back for the better part of the day, but hadn't been able to make love to the woman of his dreams.

The party was due to begin in half an hour.

"Babe, the whole team is here except for Scott, Dee, and Hiram," Clarke said.

"Clarke, I don't think Scott is going to make it."

She looked up to find a face that fought regret. She rushed across the room to embrace the lover, fiancé, expectant father, drug kingpin, employer, and executioner she had grown to love. No words were necessary. They held each other in silence.

Errol interrupted the moment by taking a look at his watch. "We should go downstairs." Then the power couple made their way down the winding staircase into a foyer filled with people, live music, and waiters with trays full of Caribbean cuisine.

As they neared the bottom of the staircase, the crowd met the couple with applause. The room was filled with the sound of drumbeats, and Errol began to dance, legs kicking and arms flailing. It felt good to see him dance through his pain. One by one he was circled by three other men who shared in the moment of jubilation, the Who's Who of the Port City. His friends were happy to see him home. However, Clarke knew they were three Kings coming to celebrate the return of one of their own.

Clarke noticed Dee as she staggered in on wobbly legs. She motioned to Tina to check on her. Minutes later Hiram entered.

The room was filled and energized by flowing drinks and drumbeats. Clarke ran to the bathroom and returned to find a slender long-legged, long-haired woman whispering to Errol. She was immediately overtaken by a wave of jealousy. As she made her way in their direction, she began to hear Errol call for everyone's attention. The room quieted, and Errol asked Clarke to join him on the stairs before the crowd.

"Clarke, you are an exceptional woman. You have supported me in ways most couldn't fathom. You have done so with style, elegance, poise, and grace. I won't imagine spending another day without you. I don't want to sound cliché, but you complete me. You are everything I'm not. From today forward, I promise to make life as simple and uncomplicated for you as I can, and as we bring our firstborn into the world, know that I strive to be a man he will always look up to." Errol wiped away the tears spilling over Clarke's eyelids. He placed his hand on her stomach and knelt to kiss it. "Clarke, words without action are pointless. As you and I build a family together, I want you to be safe and comfortable. I want you to be here."

He turned from Clarke to face the audience and said, "Please join me welcoming my fiancée to our new home."

The applause was interrupted as Dee vomited in the middle of the floor. At a nod of the head, Dee was ushered out of the room and the floor immediately cleaned. Errol leaned to Clarke and said, "Go check on your girl."

Clarke's gracious smile as she attended her guests fooled everyone. She nodded and waved at some while hugging others as she made her way to the spacious guest bathroom. She opened the door to the vanity just outside the internal part of the bathroom. Dee was slumped down in a corner chair as Tina covered her head with a cold compress, saying, "Ms. Dee, are you okay?"

"Tina, please step outside," Clarke ordered.

"Yes, ma'am," Tina replied as she walked toward the door.

"What in the hell has gotten into you, Dee?"

"What in the hell has gotten into me? No, what in the hell has gotten into you? You have changed, Clarke, and I hate the new you. You're a country girl just like me. Now all of a sudden you've risen to be someone you can't even look at in the mirror."

"We all change to fit our circumstances, Dee, and I

can look in the mirror just fine."

"Really, Clarke, can a murderer ever look herself in the mirror?"

"Murderer! What the fuck are you talking about?"

"Do you think I am that dumb, Clarke?"

"I think you're past dumb to look me in the face and accuse me of anything. Do you know who the fuck I am? I am *Mafietta*, and you'd best not forget that!"

Dee's eyes were filled with a rage Clarke had never seen before. She threw her head back and lunged forward as she spit at Clarke's feet.

"You ungrateful bitch," Clarke yelled. She hauled off and smacked Dee so hard she saw stars.

Dee stood up on wobbly legs, nose to nose with Clarke. "You killed Mike, and I know it. Forget this shit. Forget this money. I just want to sleep at night. Can you sleep at night, Clarke? Can you sleep, or have you become that cold-blooded? I am gonna prove that you killed him, and if that means going to the cops, so be it," Dee threatened.

Clarke had learned to stand her ground and was not about to fall back now. Her heart raced as Dee spewed these threats, but her demeanor never wavered as she walked even closer to her. Now their noses were touching.

"You listen, and you listen good. Here is what you are gonna do. You are gonna clean your drunk ass up, and then you are going to return to this party and act like you got some damned sense. I have always been nice to you, even when the man you claim I murdered was beating your ass, and you couldn't make the bills and the rent. So I'd advise you to remember that as you stand in my face making threats."

Clarke watched as Dee reared her hand back slowly and drunkenly, but she was faster. She pulled her baby nine millimeter and had it at Dee's temples before Dee could connect.

"I will overlook this shit *once*, Dee. You are drunk enough to let liquor speak for you, and you'd better get that shit in check."

"Are you so bold as to hold a gun to my face, Clarke, after I held you down?" Dee said as she choked on her tears. "Has Errol changed you this much?"

Clarke lowered the gun and reached over to the vanity counter and grabbed a Kleenex. She wiped Dee's tears as she said, "Once, Dee. You only get once, so you'd better make this your first and last." Clarke balled up the tissue and threw it in Dee's face, holstered her gun, and left her standing there shocked and pondering her next move.

Dee leaned to Tina and said, "Keep this bitch in the bathroom until Black comes."

"Yes, ma'am."

Black was leaning on the column just opposite the bathroom door. Since the incident months ago, he remained one of Errol's most loyal troops and was always there to assist.

"Everything okay, Clarke?" Black asked.

"Nah, take Dee somewhere to sleep off that drunk. Keep her there till Errol and I come for her."

* * *

Clarke looked down to smooth out her dress as she rounded the corner on her way to rejoin Errol. She looked up just in time to bump into Hiram.

"Hello, Hiram. I'm glad you could make it. Are you enjoying the festivities?"

"Most certainly, madame. I noticed your friend was sick. Is she okay?" He looked around the column to get a better view of the bathroom door.

"Oh, she's just fine. She just had way too much to drink." Clarke looped her arm around Hiram's and turned his focus back to the crowd. "Now, let's go see what Errol is up to," Clarke commanded slyly.

As soon as their path was clear, Clarke withdrew her

arm, and they continued to weave their way across the room.

Errol leaned over to kiss Clarke as she approached the group of troops and Kings who surrounded him.

"I saw Hiram over by the bathroom. He is quite the gentleman, I see. He had come to check on Dee. Isn't that the most chivalrous thing you've heard all evening?" Clarke asked.

"Oh, so you've taken an interest in Dee, have you?" Errol said as he and the group turned to see Hiram's reaction.

"Umm, no, not really. I just saw that she was sick and wanted to check on her. It was quite a simple and innocent gesture," Hiram replied with a voice that became shakier with every word.

"Errol, I think we should formally introduce them. You know she hasn't dated since Mike took off," Clarke suggested.

"That's not a bad idea at all, my love. We shall do it tonight. Let's give her a bit to work through her current state, though."

"Let me leave you gentlemen to talk while I make my rounds," Clarke said before politely nodding to the crowd and turning to walk away.

"I have to give it to you, Errol. Your Mafietta is quite the business-minded charmer," one King exclaimed.

"And she's done tremendous things for our profit share! She's an asset we can't afford to lose," said another.

"She is not happy with this life anymore. She wants out, guys," Errol informed the group.

"Well, that's not happening, and I hope you've advised her of that. You know how this thing works— life in and life out. She can't just quit. She knows too much."

"That's not fair," Errol retorted. "Your wives have helped us out from time to time, but they don't take an active part in the business."

"That's just it, Errol. She's not your wife."

This one's too easy, Errol thought. He would just have to push up the wedding.

***

The party was beginning to wind down and the band announced the last song of the evening, Morgan

Heritage's "She's Still Loving Me." That song carried special meaning for Errol and Clarke. More so now, than ever.

While the couple was separated by the length of the room and all the guests in between, their eyes met after the first few chords. Instinctively, as if programmed, they met each other in the middle of the floor.

For the first time since his return, Clarke was able to surrender her body to Errol's arms. The perfect fit of her head to his shoulder reassured her that despite any obstacles, he was indeed the one for her.

As the band continued to play, and the lead singer gave life to their favorite song, the couple became lost in each other and the magical moment that seemed almost mystical. Clarke came out of her trance as Errol kissed her forehead to proclaim his love.

"Clarke, we have built something special here, and there is no need to prolong things. Let's move up the wedding. We have the means to do it."

Clarke was taken aback by Errol's request, but she looked up to meet his deep and inquiring eyes and said, "When? You just got home. There's so much to do."

"Don't worry. We'll hire the best planner money can buy. You can just relax and allow them to bring your vision to life," Errol insisted.

Clarke smiled as the band played the last few notes of the song. "As you wish, my King."

Errol leaned down and planted his longing lips upon Clarke's. It sent shockwaves of desire through her body. They were both a million miles away from their guests in a universe comprised completely of their love for each other. They shared a moment so special that others stood back to admire their obvious love and were compelled to applaud. The unexpected applause broke their daze and provided a great end to a bittersweet homecoming.

And the Clock Struck Midnight

The Kings retired to the den on the right side of the foyer while Errol and Clarke stood at the door to bid each of their guests good night. As Errol closed the door behind their last visitor, Clarke removed her shoes and playfully hit Errol on the bottom.

"How did you know this was my dream house?"

"Oh, you give me no credit for being the fabulously observant man I am. I saw the vision board on your refrigerator and gave the universe a little push in making that dream come true, even down to the color of the walls and island in the kitchen."

"Stop lying," Clarke said as she punched Errol playfully in the shoulder. "You know that kitchen was for you."

"Okay, you got me." He pulled her closer. "And I can't wait to get to you. Don't you know that I've been envisioning this moment for the last four months?"

"Me, too, but business first," Clarke said as she planted a quick kiss on Errol's lips. "I'll go deal with Dee while you discuss things with the Kings. Meet you upstairs in an hour." Clarke flirted as she winked at her man.

"You got it, babe." He smacked her on the butt and

made his way to the den.

***

Dee had been sitting in a small office watching television for the last hour. She couldn't believe she had come out of the box like that. The stress of losing Mike had been weighing on her over the last few months, but she never expected her feelings to erupt like this. It was hard to see past her headache and the haze remaining from the "loud" she'd just smoked, but she remembered threatening Clarke with the cops and then a gun being in her face.

She had to fix this. Clarke didn't take kindly to disloyalty, and she knew it. Hell, everyone who did business with her knew it. She looked over at the chair beside her. Black was watching *The Jeffersons* contentedly.

He looked over to Dee and said, "This couple cracks me up. That short guy is so funny parading around with that walk."

However, Dee didn't feel like being a part of the small talk. She got the feeling her life may be at stake.

Just then Arvin opened the door and announced,

"Dee, Clarke is here to see you."

Dee swallowed hard, straightened up in her chair. . She sat with her hands clasped together in her lap and prepared herself for whatever fate might befall her. Black stood up, and Clarke replaced him in the chair beside Dee.

Clarke faced Dee squarely but said nothing. She sat and allowed her eyes to bore a hole into Dee's spirit. Then, after what seemed like an eternity to Dee but was really about a minute, Clarke spoke. "Dee, how are you feeling, now? She turned to Arvin and ordered, "Get Dee a couple Tylenol and a glass of water."

"I am feeling much better now, Clarke. I am not sure what got into me out there. I'm happy for you and Errol. I really am, but I think the thought of you guys moving on and having a baby—and him buying you this house—just got to me. I used to have dreams like this. I dreamed Mike and I would have the perfect life, with a brick house—not as big as this, but a nice one—with a picket fence and couple of kids running around. Only now, my prince charming has vanished without a trace, and no one can tell me what happened. Can you imagine what that feels like, Clarke? Trade places with me for a second. Can you feel the weight of my heart?"

A single tear formed and hung on Clarke's right eyelash. It fell as she began to speak. "Dee, I fought that feeling every day Errol was locked up. Wondering if he would make it home safely, if the Feds would let him go, what in the world we would do when he did make it home. While I can't say I know what you're going through, I can relate to the sentiment."

A look of relief crossed Dee's face as Clarke continued to speak. "But let's not get things confused. My heart goes out to you, Dee, but if you ever speak to me like that again, there won't be another conversation. We didn't get to where we are in this business by being pushovers. I don't take kindly to threats of the police, and to be honest, you of all people shouldn't be making them, because if you inspect the situation closely, I am only guilty of owning several successful salons, barber shops, properties, and of being an avid financial supporter in the campaigns of our local district attorney, and a couple of local judges. You, on the other hand, touch cocaine. You pick it up, deliver it, and then bring the proceeds from it to me as rent and percentages from the barbers and stylists who work in these shops. My hands, my dear, are clean." Clarke leaned in to get in

Dee's face. "Yours, on the other hand, not so much."

That's when the truth hit Dee in the face like a ton of bricks. She was being set up to be the fall guy. She sobered up real quick as she considered the possibility of her future. She had one chance to get out, and his name was Officer Vincent Rouche.

Arvin entered with a small green pill bottle, the same one he found buried under a coffee filter and grounds in Clarke's trash can.

Dee saw the bottle and immediately realized that she'd been found out. Her leg took on a life of its own and began to bounce up and down. However, this calming mechanism wasn't much of a help this time.

Arvin handed Clarke the bottle and the glass of water.

"It seems I had a couple of these myself earlier today and thank you. I was able to get some much-needed rest. Now, it's my turn to return the favor." She shook two pills into the top of the bottle and handed it to Dee.

Damn, Dee thought. *This bitch is thorough.* She instinctively took the pills labeled "Ambien" and followed with the glass of water.

"Of course, we wouldn't want you to drive home like this, so we'll just have you stay here tonight." Clarke turned to Black and continued, "Let's hold on to Dee's cellphone for the night as well. We wouldn't want her to be disturbed."

Dee was fuming with anger and frustration but knew better than to say a word. She was stuck and had to play the game. Hopefully, she would come out alive.

"Black will show you to your room and hang out in there with you, just to make sure you don't need anything. We wouldn't want you to get hungry or thirsty and not be able to find the kitchen, so consider him your butler for the night. There are some fresh pajamas on the bed. Throw your clothes outside the door once you get downstairs, and we'll get them all washed up and fresh for you to wear home tomorrow."

The conversation gave Dee some solace. Clarke said she'd be going home tomorrow; she just hoped it wasn't home to Jesus.

Clarke got up and extended her arms to Dee. Dee stood up slowly as she began to feel the effects of the Ambien kick in.

"Black, please show Dee to her room," Clarke said.

"I'll send some popcorn up a little later to help absorb that alcohol. After all, the show is about to start," Clarke said matter-of-factly.

As Black began to lead Dee out of the room, Clarke said, "Don't forget to grab her clothes. We want them all clean for her in the morning."

Black closed the door behind him, and Arvin said, "Cuz, excuse my expression, but you're one cold bitch."

"Well, cuzzo, I've learned to live with regret," Clarke replied.

Arvin shook his head as they finished an episode of *The Jeffersons*.

Clarke stood up and stretched, ready to get to the arms of her man. Rocko came in with Dee's clothes.

Arvin began by checking the pants pocket, but only found a few twenties and a bag of weed. He moved to her blazer and pulled out a crumpled business card. He handed it to Clarke.

She took one look at the card she had designed just a couple days earlier and began to laugh. "Well, guys, we're one step closer to getting rid of her ass. She took the bait."

Arvin and Rocko smiled as Clarke walked toward the door. They began to sing the theme song they privately taunted her with. "Her name is Mafietta, Mafietta."

"Shut up, guys. Love y'all and see ya in the a.m."

***

Meanwhile, Errol and the Kings were dealing with issues of their own.

"Yo, man, it crushes my spirit to hear about Scott, man," Nigel, one of the Kings, began.

"It broke my heart to do it. Do you know what it was like to dead a childhood friend? We grew up together shoeless and hungry running along streets filled with red clay begging for change to buy a soda," Errol countered.

"No need for sentiment now. He was a thief, and thieves are dealt with. The rest is irrelevant. You two need to hit your reset buttons and keep it moving," Admiral advised.

Errol walked to the cabinet and pulled out glasses for everyone. He poured each of them a shot of rum. He held up his glass and proposed a toast. "Here's to more money, more happiness, and no regrets."

The men cheered, and each man gulped down a shot of numbing liquid.

Admiral gave the men a moment to reflect on friends lost, money made, and sorrows felt before directing them to the task at hand. "Errol, we must give you credit—your lady is business-minded and fierce. She stepped up like we never believed she could when you were away. She even tripled your profit. For that we are grateful, but this increase is not without consequence. Now we must deal with unwanted eyes and interrogations. The cops were able to lock up a King. This has never happened before, and we must make sure it never happens again."

"I think Clarke had a good thought when she required our partners to have legitimate businesses through which to funnel their proceeds. Everyone is current on their state and federal taxes, so for now, things display a picture of legitimacy for us all," Errol explained.

"What do you plan to do with Clarke now that you are back?" Nigel inquired.

Errol smiled as he thought of his plans for a future with Clarke. "I plan to have her go back to being normal. She has done all that I asked. She created a solid foundation for continued success far into the future. For now, I just want her to focus on taking care of herself, planning our wedding, and having a healthy child."

Errol observed as the Kings looked at each other exchanging nervous glances. "Do you have opposing thoughts?" Errol asked.

Reluctantly Admiral replied, "Do you have any idea how much she increased business? I'm afraid we have grown to lean on her expertise these last few months. Mandell isn't ready to let her go."

The room quieted as Errol poured himself another drink and sank deep into his plush sitting chair facing the other Kings. The room was filled with anxious bodies awaiting Errol's rebuttal to this obviously touchy subject. It wasn't often that Mandell concerned himself with their day-to-day activities, and the entire room knew it.

Errol felt the room looking to him for an answer and carefully constructed his next statement. "As you all know; Clarke is with child—my child. As I see it, nothing is more important than allowing her to move away from this stress-filled way of life long enough to take care of herself and our little one. She is exceptional when it comes to numbers and pointing out anomalies. We shall limit her role to that of an accountant of sorts. I am back, and there is no need to vex her further. I trust that you will relay that fact to Mandell for me, my brother." Errol looked to Admiral for a response.

"I will gladly relay that message. I think your response is more than fair."

"Now, if there is no objection from my fellow Kings, I'd like to properly celebrate my homecoming." Errol walked across the room to the credenza, opened the cabinet door, and pulled out a spliff. He lit it and inhaled deeply.

He needed to take this all in right now. Mandell had something up his sleeve. There was no need to keep Clarke on actively within the business. He exhaled, thinking of his own plan.

The mood lightened as the herb made its way around the room. The conversation quickly changed to memories of their childhood and reports of their wives and children.

For the time being, they were just men.

***

After about half an hour of screaming, laughing, and jovial conversation, Errol interrupted. "Gentlemen, you'll have to excuse me. I haven't seen my woman in over four months, and you know what time it is."

The room began to taunt Errol and give bedroom advice.

"Damn, that's gonna be some good shit. You've been gone for four months, and she's pregnant," Nigel remarked.

"When you feel the pressure coming, you betta slow down, or hell, stop altogether. You wouldn't want to have your internal celebration before she did," Barker, another King joked.

"Don't you worry about me. I got this," Errol said.

"Oh, do you?" Admiral asked teasingly.

"Yep, I'm gonna wear a condom," Errol replied jokingly.

Suddenly the room was filled with laughter. The gentlemen gathered their blazers. They all exchanged hugs as the Kings retired to their rooms in Errol's newest acquisition.

Admiral was the last to leave. As Errol hugged his

brother, he whispered into his ear. "Mandell is up to something. Let's discuss it in the morning."

Admiral nodded and made his way down the hall of the guest wing with the other Kings. Errol took the stairs to his bedroom suite two at a time.

Magic Moments

Errol and his humongous smile opened the door to the bedroom he and his future wife would share from now on. He entered the perfectly decorated room. The Estruscan red walls gave the room a relaxing feel, and the chartreuse and stony-ground accents in the wall paintings and vases brought the tranquil and refreshing environment to life.

Errol walked past the California king-size bed and through the bedroom sitting area that offered the same inviting and calming feel, to the bathroom where he found Clarke with the wall stereo blaring Tarrus Riley's "Far Away."

Errol laughed as Clarke tried to sing. "When I'm far, faraway; she always waits. Even when I'm far, faraway, she never gives my love away!"

He removed his shirt and stepped out of his pants. He quickly removed his boxers and quietly opened the steam-coated shower door.

Clarke didn't hear him as he joined her in the shower. He wrapped his arms around her bulging stomach and began to comfortingly lather the suds that cascaded down her body.

His hands slowly and methodically moved up to her chest where he massaged underneath her breasts. Clarke exclaimed a sigh of relief and sank farther into his arms. His hands moved upward and kneaded her breasts, never touching her nipples.

Her body was simply reacting now, but Clarke held in her screams. The water from the hot shower was not the only thing running down her leg as Errol finally began to caress her erect nipples. She tried to turn around to kiss him, but he wouldn't allow it.

"You've been so strong for so long. Let me pleasure you for now," Errol lovingly commanded.

He leaned down to nibble at her ears as his hands moved down her chest, over the stomach bearing his child, down to her triangle. He massaged her thighs, first on the outer sides and then moved to her inner thighs.

Clarke lost control of her body as her legs widened, asking Errol to explore the spot impatiently waiting to meet him. He ignored her body's request and continued to stroke her thighs. She moaned, inviting him to explore deeper.

The bulging rod poking her in the back was a

testament to the restraint Errol had as he continued to thrill her. His hands moved from her inner thigh to her lower lips. His hands manipulated them in slow circular motions, stimulating her clitoris even more. His unrelenting hands moved inward to finally address the heat that had been eagerly awaiting him.

Clarke called out in ecstasy as her lover began to use his fingers to manipulate and stimulate her. The months of not being touched told on her, and she yelled out within seconds as she climaxed. Errol refused to give her relief as his hands moved down to the spot that called out to him from the moment he entered the shower.

As his fingers entered her warm dark place, Clarke's breathing intensified even more. She felt his rod begin to throb as he explored her depths, and finally she saw room to take control. She quickly turned and began to stroke Errol and his ego as they kissed, and she pushed him toward the bench on the back wall of the shower.

However, Errol didn't miss a beat, and his fingers quickly found their initial spot as the palm of his hand continued to send waves of heat through her body. Errol lowered himself onto the bench as Clarke began to suck his bottom lip.

She mounted her mate and engulfed him in a sea of warm and wet juices. Clarke began slowly, watching the look of ecstasy now covering Errol's face. It was her time to turn things up. She moved up and down, up and down, faster and faster as his hands held on to her breasts.

The moans that now filled the shower belonged to Errol. His hands moved down her body and held on to her waist as she felt him throb within her. Clarke wrapped her hands caressingly around Errol's head and began to plunge her tongue into the depths of his mouth as his moans became increasingly loud.

Once the tremors stopped, their eyes met. They both knew this was a love to fight for. Errol lifted Clarke, stood, and held her hand as they moved back into the full stream of the water. He lathered her body lovingly, and she turned to do the same for him.

They both laughed as they stepped hurriedly from the shower. Clarke quickly wrapped herself in a towel and grabbed another as she began to kiss and dry the droplets of water from Errol's back. He turned, and she did the same for his chest. She finished and handed him the towel.

"I believe my work is done here." She laughed.

"Oh really?" Errol inquired as he wrapped the towel around his waist, reached for Clarke's hand, and led her to their bedroom.

"Oh, my God, Errol! I love our bedroom. It is so beautiful," Clarke said.

Errol turned down the sheets and helped Clarke crawl into bed. "This was your vision, babe. I just looked at your boards and made it happen."

"There's just one thing, Errol. Where is the television?"

Errol laughed as he pushed a button on one of the remotes and a TV began to rise out of the stand at the bottom of the bed.

"You pulled out all the stops, didn't you, Mr. Bellow?"

"Anything for you, Mafietta," Errol said jokingly.

Clarke grabbed one of the pillows and swatted Errol across the face.

He reached out and pulled her down to him on the bed.

Neither of them knew when they fell asleep, but they were sent hurtling back to reality as they woke to a knock on their door.

Back to Reality

"What?!" Clarke and Errol screamed at the same time.

A nervous Rocko peeked his head around the door and said, "Clarke, Dee is up and ready to leave."

"That can't be the reason you just came in here and woke us up, Rocko. What time is it? Eight or nine?" Clarke asked.

Rocko laughed. "No, man, it's almost two in the afternoon."

Clarke turned to look at Errol. They both laughed, shaking their heads.

"Did I put it down like that, babe?" Clarke asked Errol jokingly.

"Uhm," Rocko interjected loudly. "I'm still standing here."

"Well, get out!" Errol responded playfully.

"Have you forgotten that the Kings are still here, too?" Rocko reminded the couple.

"Let them know we'll be down shortly, and have Jeanette start breakfast," Errol said as he sat up in the bed.

"Rocko, will you bring me up some crackers and ginger ale, please? I think it's gonna be one of those days."

Rocko lightheartedly rolled his eyes up in his head and closed the door.

Now, with the room emptied, Errol leaned over and kissed Clarke passionately on the lips. "Good morning, sunshine."

"Good morning, babe."

"Wanna come join me for a shower?" Errol asked suggestively.

"I'd love to, but if my feet touch the floor before I get something on my stomach, you'll see the true meaning of morning sickness." Clarke said as she wrapped her arms around her man.

They enjoyed the embrace they'd missed for so long. Their eyes were closed when another knock hit the door.

"Yes," Errol said.

The door opened, and it was Admiral.

"What are you doing up here, man?"

"I wanted you to bring me up to speed before we meet with the rest of the Kings," Admiral responded to his brother. "I didn't want to raise suspicion by speaking to you alone once you made it downstairs."

"No worries, let's go in the sitting room," Errol said as he pointed to the area adjoining the bedroom.

Admiral went to take a seat as Errol passed Clarke her robe. Rocko reappeared with crackers, apple slices, cheese, peanut butter, and ginger ale.

Clarke thankfully accepted the tray. She took a few sips of the ginger ale and slowly chewed a few of the apple slices.

Rocko stood between Clarke and the sitting area as she placed her arms into the robe. She tied the belt, grabbed a few more apple and cheese slices, and turned to join her family.

"So how did things go last night?" Admiral asked of Clarke once she sat down.

"Just as we planned. Dee took the bait. We found Officer Rouche's business card in her pocket."

"What exactly is the plan here?" Errol asked.

Clarke looked lovingly to her fiancé and began to explain. "I was sure to keep my hands clean while you were away. Dee became my voice, and I just pulled the strings. Now, considering all the unmarked cars swarming around the restaurant, I think it's time that someone take a fall. Literally and figuratively."

"Damn, you're cold-blooded!" Admiral exclaimed.

"I have a family to protect," Clarke responded possessively.

"I like her style." Admiral chuckled. "Now, how did things work out with Hiram?" he asked, turning to Errol.

"He did the same. Our actor is performing well. Hiram believes he and Officer Rouche are going extort a great deal of money from us before stealing a shipment and sending us all to prison."

Errol shook his head as he rose. "Damn, money changes everything, don't it?"

"Money doesn't make a man a monster. The person within does. Money merely magnifies the mirror, if you're a good man, you become a better one," Admiral responded. He walked toward the door, and

Rocko followed. He turned to the couple and said, "Now will you please get dressed. We know Errol just got home, and it's been a while, but heaven's sake, it's almost three."

"See you in twenty minutes," Errol said as he watched their most loyal partners exit the room.

"There went my plans for the shower," Errol said with the sad face.

"No worries, there is always tonight," Clarke said as she walked toward the bathroom. "Let's get this over with, so we can christen every room in this place." Clarke winked as Errol stood to join her.

This time, Errol and Clarke turned on their individual shower jets to wash away all the love left from the night before.

"I love this two-shower-head idea. You were really looking out. Thanks, babe."

"Anything for my queen," Errol responded with pride.

Errol and Clarke dressed hurriedly and met the group in the dining room as they were filling plates with stacks of fruit, hotcakes, bacon, and other items. "So, you two finally decided to join us," Nigel said flippantly.

"Yep!" replied Errol. He pulled out Clarke's chair to the right of his seat at the head of the table.

Brunch was filled with lighthearted conversation and tons of laughter.

When the plates of their guests were nearly empty, Errol posed a question that shocked the crowd. "Clarke and I need to take some time to get reacquainted and plan our wedding. I have been away for months, and I need a vacation." Errol turned to Hiram. "Hiram, would you mind overseeing things for me? I'll be here for meetings, but I need you to oversee the day-to-day operations for the next couple of weeks."

Hiram quickly responded, "Sure thing, Errol, anything you need."

Clarke turned to Dee and presented the same offer. "Would you do the same?"

Dee reluctantly agreed. Her thoughts went to the officer who had stopped her the previous night, but then again, if she put him off for two weeks, she could make some stupid money before sending the Bellow family off to reservations at the penitentiary.

"Are you okay, Dee?" Clarke asked. "You responded a bit slower than I expected."

"Oh, I'm sorry, Clarke. I am just humbled that you would still allow me to work."

"You have to eat, don't you?" Clarke asked.

"You got it!" Dee responded. A smile covered her face as she thought, *She's given me a chance to redeem myself. This means I can stay alive while I dig all of their graves.*

Errol and the Kings retired to his den for cognac and cigars as Clarke walked Dee to the door.

"Thanks, Clarke," Dee said, unable to look her in the face.

"Thanks for what?" Clarke asked.

"Thanks for giving me a second chance. I was real drunk last night, and—"

Clarke interrupted her, "No worries. That's all water over the bridge. Let's get this money," Clarke said as she hugged Dee.

For a second, Dee almost felt guilty for turning on her friends. However, the sentiment didn't last.

She was off to dig ditches.

The Tribulations of Wedding Planning

"Errol, how in the world can we plan a wedding in two weeks?" Clarke asked.

"Don't worry, babe. I already have it taken care of," Errol confidently responded.

"Taken care of—what do you mean? You can't plan a wedding without the bride!" Clarke said.

"Calm down, love. I simply mean that I hired a planner," Errol replied.

"I hope you didn't hire some hood booger passing herself off as a planner," Clarke said jokingly.

"What a shot to the heart. You give me no credit. If you had to choose the best planner in the city, who would you choose?"

"I would have called Eliza-Beth Rushing."

Errol stood there and smiled as he waited on his fiancée to realize that he'd just gotten the best planner in town to plan their wedding in just two weeks.

Clarke covered her mouth and began to jump up and down. "Baby, did you get Eliza-Beth Rushing?" she screamed joyfully. "Oh my God, you got her. How'd you do it? How much did it cost? When are we meeting? Oh, shit, I gotta get an outfit!"

Errol closed the gap between him and the mouth moving a million miles a minute. He wrapped his arms around his future wife and said, "She'll be here on Monday morning at ten."

"Ah, you are amazing! I love you so much," Clarke said as she stood on her tiptoes to give her man a kiss on the lips. She expected a quick peck in return, but the passion that met her nearly sent her head spinning.

Errol stabilized her by placing his hand behind her head. He wove his hands into the strands of her hair and poured his love into her through that kiss.

"Wow! That was powerful," Clarke said as she tried to regain her bearings.

"No, babe, that's what real love feels like, and I'm not done yet." He took Clarke's hand and led her up the stairs to their bedroom.

***

Dee's mind raced for the entire length of her drive home. Her head was still throbbing from last night's indiscretions. Questions invaded her head. What if someone saw her with Officer Rouche? This could mean the end for her. What if things went down just as he promised? Did she really have the heart to set them all up? Dee had never felt as tired, scared, and paranoid as she did right then.

The pros and cons of her current situation weighed heavily as Dee stepped out of her car and walked to her front door, key in hand. She reached out to touch the door with her fob. To her surprise, the door swung open as the weight of her hand connected with it.

Dee snapped back to reality. She pushed the door open and said, "Who's in here? Come out now, or I'll shoot."

Dee quickly reached her hand in the large vase beside the door and pulled out her baby 380. She began to wave it slowly around the room as she attempted to assess the scene. "Who is in here?" Dee screamed. She saw a tall muscular figure coming from her bedroom with a photo album in his hand.

It was Officer Rouche. "Calm down. Calm down," he

said. "It's just me."

"What the hell are you doing in my apartment?"

"Oh, Dee. I expected a much warmer welcome. I let you walk away from about four or five different infractions last night. And this is how you treat me?"

Dee kicked the front door closed with her foot and laid her gun on the counter. "What do you want from me?"

"I want this Mafietta and her boyfriend who calls himself a King. It's time the Bellow brothers and the Kings know they aren't so untouchable," Vincent Rouche responded.

"Are you asking me to snitch on them, Officer Rouche?" Dee asked.

"Don't call me Officer Rouche. Call me Vincent. That's much less formal. Yes, I do want you to fill me in on the intricacies of their business so the Port City PD can clean up the streets. Who knows, the Feds may even become involved. You just have to tell me exactly what we are dealing with," he said as he tried to seem less threatening.

Dee took a deep breath and walked into the kitchen. Vincent seemed a little unnerved as she opened her cabinet, but he showed relief once she pulled out a glass and a bottle of Hennessey. She poured herself a shot and gulped it down all at once. She wiped her mouth with the back of her hand and said, "I know what you're asking me to do, and I'm ready."

Vincent Rouche could barely believe his luck. He expected to have to pull and tug at Dee for cooperation. He never believed this would be so easy.

"Would you like a drink?" Dee asked, now that she had the bit of courage she needed.

"Sure, I'll take a double." He sat in the corner of her brown leather sectional couch and faced the kitchen.

"What do you want to know?" Dee asked.

"I want to know everything. I want to know how it started, how you became a part of this organization, but most important, I want to know how they move."

Dee poured them both drinks and reached back in the cabinet for a small box filled with prerolled blunts. She grabbed one, closed the box, closed the cabinet, grabbed both drinks, and plopped down on the couch next to Vincent.

"Where do you want to begin?" Dee asked.

"At the beginning, as you know it, will be fine. Do you mind if I tape this just so I have a record of our conversations?"

"Why do you need to tape this?" Dee asked reluctantly as the small quiet sound of fire touching tobacco took up the small fragile space between them. She took a deep drag on the cigar, threw her head back, and allowed the smoke to run from her lungs back to the atmosphere.

"I am gonna tape this to make sure we leave no stone unturned as we take Mafietta and the King down. I want to make sure that we nail her little arrogant ass to the wall."

Dee nodded, pleased with his response.

A small click filled the silence as Vincent pressed the record button on his handheld recorder. He began, "This is a personal interview with Ms. Deshaunda Teal. Dee, is it okay to record our conversation here today?"

"Yes."

"Is it also okay to use this tape as a means to prosecute the elusive woman known to us as

Mafietta?" he said.

"Yes it is," Dee said as she lay back into the softness of the leather and crossed her legs underneath her in the seat. "What do you need to know?"

Vincent pulled out a tablet and pen and began to write as he bombarded Dee with questions. Three hours later, he stood to his feet and said, "I think I have enough to get started. Do you have any questions for me?"

"I have one request. Can we get this bitch on her wedding day? It isn't fair that she gets to walk down the aisle, marry the man of her dreams, and live this amazing life when she poisoned every piece of happiness I ever tried to have."

"What about her baby, don't you want to wait until after her baby is born?"

"Hell no!" Dee thought of the twins she'd lost. She took a deep pull on the blunt and continued, "If you do the crime, you pay the time, right?"

"You're absolutely right," Vincent said as he threw back the rest of his drink and walked toward the door. "We'll speak soon." He quietly closed the door behind him.

***

Vincent dialed a number and placed his phone on his shoulder as he reached to turn the ignition of his Dodge Charger.

The deep voice on the other end of the phone answered, "Yep, what's up?"

"She took the bait: hook, line, and sinker. Someone must have really pissed her off," Vincent responded.

"Great news. Keep up the good work."

"Oh boss, one more thing. She wants the take down to be on May eighth."

"The wedding day?"

"Yep, she's wrathful," Vincent replied.

"Well, that's not quite the bang I'd planned, but the timing couldn't be better. Let's roll with it."

"You got it, boss." Vincent responded just before the phone went click, and the voice was gone.

Vincent shuddered as he pulled away. He was off to meet Hiram for a late lunch. These were some really messed-up people.

***

Clarke and Errol began their Saturday morning at Barnes & Noble. They bought every bridal magazine on the rack, loaded up on every planning book in sight, and bought two editions of Emily Post's book of *Etiquette*.

Their arms were filled with bags of books as they walked happily to the car. Clarke had her man back. He was the normal, surefooted, confident man she'd fallen in love with. That made all the other headaches minimal ones for now. The happy couple decided to grab some take out at Romano's Macaroni Grill before heading home.

Clarke left the books and wobbled to the bathroom as Errol and Lil' Stupid brought them in and dropped them on the massive dining-room table. Errol set out the food on the other end of the table and poured himself a glass of rum and some ginger ale for Clarke.

She returned moments later to join him. The couple spent the next half hour laughing as Clarke tried to explain all of the crazy things that happened while Errol was away.

"I didn't know I had it in me," Clarke said.

"No one does," Errol responded. "Sometimes you don't even realize what you've become until you look up one day and see all of the sadness in your eyes and weight on your shoulders."

He took a bite of his steak and looked to his fiancée. Instead of finding understanding eyes, he found ones filled with tears.

Clarke was crying. He quickly walked over to her and immediately lifted her into his lap. He held her tightly in his arms as he wiped away the bucket of tears that streamed down her face.

Clarke was broken and in pain. This was the first time Errol felt how much. He could actually feel her. He felt the heaviness of her spirit. He felt the fear masked by strength. He felt the stress and anxiety, and for the first time he realized that he'd almost ruined a great woman.

Clarke felt the sadness and regret that began to consume Errol, so she quickly wiped her eyes and composed herself. She turned slowly to passionately kiss Errol on the mouth. He was taken by surprise as Clarke's new positive energy pulsated through his body.

He held her tighter, pulled away from her mouth,

and began to plant kisses down her neck. He wrapped one hand around the back of her head as the other moved through her hair, down her neck, and tenderly onto her chest.

Errol leaned in to kiss Clarke again as Lil' Stupid walked in the dining room waving a torn page from a bridal magazine. "Yo, Errol, I like this—"

Lil' Stupid stopped cold in his tracks when he saw that his boss was busy, but it was too late.

Errol gave Clarke a quick peck on the cheek and sat her up in his lap. Both of them smiling.

"You like this, what?" Clarke asked.

"I like this tux! This is wicked. I want to wear this one."

"And who told you that you were even in the wedding?" Clarke asked jokingly.

"Well, I just kinda thought that you guys would want me to stand front and center with you, since I do kinda take care of y'all." Lil' Stupid said bashfully.

Errol let out a hearty laugh and responded, "Steve, we wouldn't have it any other way. Now let me see that picture."

Clarke and Errol spent hours leafing through the pages of bridal magazines. By the time the clock struck ten, they had tuxedos, bridesmaid dresses, flowers, decorations, invites, and two cakes all picked out.

Now all they had to do was show Eliza-Beth the vision, and she could work out the rest.

Not Quite Soul Food Sunday

Errol invited the entire crew over for Sunday dinner. The kitchen was filled with smells of both Jamaican and southern home cooking. Anna, the cook, was setting the table as the doorbell rang. Their first guest had arrived. Errol opened the heavy rustic door as he looked through the side panel of glass. Dee and Tina were standing with bottles of wine in their hands.

"We brought you something special!" Tina exclaimed as Errol opened the door for the pair.

"Thank you. We'll have it with dinner," Errol said as he stepped aside and the ladies entered. Before he could close the door, he saw two cars pulling up. Most of the gang was there now. Hiram was the only one missing. The group exchanged small talk in Errol's den as Anna prepared the table.

Moments later they were sitting at a table filled with the soul food everyone loved. There was the quiet buzz of conversation when the doorbell rang again.

This time, Jeanette went to the door. She announced, "Mr. Hiram is here." Then she showed him to his seat at the table.

Hiram sat next to Dee in the only available chair. He glanced over at Dee as he pulled the chair out from the table. He saw her cleavage bulging from the top of her shirt. Her hair flowed down her back, and it was all hers. There were no lines from sewn-in tracks. He was impressed. He leaned over and whispered a quick, "Hello, beautiful!"

Dee looked up and smiled as she said, "Hello. And you are?" She batted her eyelashes as she stuck out her hand.

He shook the hand she extended and kissed it.

"Wow," Dee said. "Chivalry isn't dead."

"No it isn't. I'm Hiram. It's great to formally meet you." Hiram realized that working with Dee wouldn't be so bad.

"Um-hmm." The sound snapped them both out of their trance.

Hiram looked to Errol and said, "Man, you didn't tell me my new partner was so beautiful."

"This isn't the first time you've met, Hiram." Tina interjected.

"I know. I don't know how I missed her the first time. Maybe it was the way you whisked her off to bed, but I have my sights set now!"

Dee held her head down to hide the Kool-Aid smile covering her mouth. This was the first time she'd looked at another man sexually since Mike disappeared. She felt that dating again would somehow taint his memory, but that feeling was beginning to pass.

Everyone could see the sparks between Dee and Hiram flying high. For a second, Clarke almost felt bad for placing Dee in such a predicament, but then her thoughts raced back to Dee's threats at Errol's party. Her loyalty was now questionable, and that was the end of it.

Clarke shook her head as she came back to reality. "Baby, would you say grace?" she asked Errol.

Everyone bowed their heads as Errol prayed over the food and for their continued safety.

After the amen, the room was filled with the sounds of serving spoons hitting the sides of Pyrex dishes as everyone made their plates.

At this moment, they were all family again. He wasn't the leader, and they weren't his troops. They were just family. Then the pangs of the truth stabbed Errol in the heart. He sat pondering ways to avoid the impending punishment, but the Kings had decided, and there was no turning back now.

Errol thought back to the Jay-Z song "Regrets," and he reclaimed the burden that came with being the head of the Bellow family. He snapped back to a table filled with laughter.

"What were you thinking about, Boss?" Lil' Stupid asked.

The question caught Errol off his guard, but he responded simply, "I'm thinking of Judas and Jesus."

A hush fell on the table but was quickly alleviated when Clarke said, "I snuck down here this morning and made a three-layer pound cake. Any takers?"

The room responded with a resounding, "YES!"

She placed her hand on Errol's thigh and gave him a quick kiss on the forehead as she got up to get dessert plates.

Moments later, dinner napkins began to hit the various plates as the group finished their cake.

Errol, wanting to savor the moment, said, "Anyone

up for soccer?"

The men immediately agreed.

"I was hoping you'd say that!" Black exclaimed. "I have my sneakers in the car."

Within seconds the men were leaving the table.

"Hey, Black, no cryin' like last time, dude," Errol teased.

"Man, you cheated," Black responded.

Looking at these men interact together reminded Clarke of the reasons she was so dedicated to saving them and preserving her newfound family.

Clarke's phone began to ring. It was Reverend Dubois.

***

"Clarke, I love you with all my heart, but we're gonna have to find a new pastor to marry us. I don't do counseling. It reminds me too much of an interrogation," Errol said.

"Errol, marriage counseling is a common thing here. Reverend Dubois just wants to make sure that we love each other and want God in our marriage," Clarke explained.

"He should know that I wouldn't have it any other way. I don't need him in our business. I just need him to marry us," Errol said.

"It won't kill you to meet with the pastor, Errol."

"I told you I don't believe in counseling, Clarke." Errol repeated.

"Really, Errol. Is it that serious?"

"You damned right it is. He can't just force this on us. We can just get someone else to marry us," Errol retorted.

"He is the leader of that church, and he can do as he pleases." Clarke sounded aggravated.

"We'll just find another church, then. I am not going to counseling, babe. We are just fine, and we don't need it. Do I make myself clear?" Errol asked in a superior tone.

"Errol, at this point, I don't give a damn what you have to say," Clarke said. Her voice began to get louder. "You will have your black ass in the pastor's study tomorrow morning at eleven, and I mean it.

Don't test me with this one, Errol." Clarke's voice trembled.

A tear was frozen on her eyelash. Errol saw it and immediately felt guilty for putting Clarke through this stress.

"I'll go, I'll go," he said. "Just don't cry. I'll do whatever it takes, just don't cry."

Clark smiled at her future husband. He wrapped his arms around her and said, "Clarke, I will do anything you ask. I love you."

He leaned in and passionately kissed away all of Clarke's stresses. "I'll handle the meeting with the pastor from here. Give me his number, and I'll firm up tomorrow's meeting with him."

Clarke sent Errol the contact from her phone and smiled as he dialed Reverend Dubois's number. She decided to go upstairs and run a bath. She gave Errol a quick peck on the cheek and headed for the bedroom.

This Sunday had been an exhausting one for Clarke. Her stomach was growing larger every day, and so was her appetite. Her feet and ankles had minds of their own, and she had to trade in her stilettos for flats and wedges. Right now, though, all she wanted was a warm, sudsy bath.

***

Clarke's eyes opened as Errol lifted her out of the cold water surrounding her. The warm soapy liquid must have lulled her to sleep. Errol slowly dried her off with a towel.

He began at her shoulders and slowly wiped down to the curve of her buttocks. In one quick motion, he'd wrapped the towel around her body and was now massaging Clarke's breasts through the towel. She let out a soft moan. Errol kneaded one of her breasts as he flicked the nipple of the other one with his tongue. His other hand traveled down her chest, over her belly button, past her bulging stomach, and down to her perfectly manicured mound. Two fingers traced the insides of her lips sending a bolt of pleasure pulsating through Clarke's body. His fingers reached her opening, but rubbed over it despite Clarke's desire to have him plunge them deep within her.

He moved his hands back and forth over the spot until he had opened the dam inside her. Clarke's clit was throbbing. She wanted him so badly. And by the look of things, he wanted her, too. Errol was steady and ready down there, but he pushed away Clarke's hand as she reached for his pole.

In a swift motion, he picked her up again. He walked through the sitting area and laid Clarke softly on the bed. Errol straddled his future wife and began to plant kisses on her neck. He moved slowly to her breasts. He suckled one until Clarke let out a room-filling moan that urged him to continue his travels to a lower destination.

Errol moved his kisses lower. He kissed the protruding tummy that housed his son as his hands slowly opened Clarke's legs. Errol wasted no time as his tongue delved into her sweet spot. Clarke screamed as Errol's tongue circled her button and dipped in and out of her honey hole.

She felt the bed underneath her become wet and slippery as Errol continued to pleasure her. Clarke was beginning to climax when Errol entered her. Her pulsating tunnel quickly wrapped itself tightly around his shaft. He exclaimed, "Woman, I love you," and he kissed her passionately on the lips. Their bodies were one as Clarke wrapped her legs around Errol's waist to help him find her deep fleshy place. He did, and they both begin to moan loudly as their movements complemented each other, and their bodies found synchronization.

Clarke could feel Errol's pole throbbing as he filled her. He moved a hand down below and began to rub her man in the boat faster and faster. His hips did the same. Suddenly the room was filled with the sound of them both.

Clarke wiped tears from her right eye as Errol kissed them away on her left. "Why are you crying?" he asked.

"Do you really need to ask?" Clarke jokingly responded.

"Nah, not really." Errol laughed.

"Babe, would you run downstairs and grab me some ice cream with cinnamon apples and wet walnuts on top?"

"Sure, love," Errol responded. He grabbed and tied his robe as he headed toward the door.

"I love you!" Clarke called out to Errol.

"I love you, too!" Errol responded as he closed the door behind him.

Clarke fell back into the down-stuffed pillows that covered the head of their bed. She closed her eyes to relive the passionate moment she and Errol had just shared, but she heard a vibration on the nightstand. She reached over to check the caller identification on her phone.

"Good evening, Reverend Dubois," Clarke said.

"Good evening, Sister Clarke, I just wanted you to share something with Brother Errol for me. Please let him know that I've considered his offer, and while the church could definitely use a new bus, I don't feel that his buying one should be a valid reason to not attend marriage counseling."

"Are you saying that Errol tried to bribe you?"

"I'm afraid so," Pastor Dubois replied hesitantly.

"Don't worry, Reverend Dubois, we'll be there tomorrow for counseling, and we'll still see about getting that bus for the church. How does that sound?" Clarke asked.

"That will be great, Sister Clarke. I'll see you both tomorrow," Reverend Dubois said before hanging up.

"ERROL!" Clarke screamed.

He was halfway up the stairs when he heard Clarke screaming his name. He ran to see what the yelling was about. "What is it, babe?" Errol asked with a concerned look.

The smell of warm apples filled the room, and Clarke stuck out her hand to get the ice cream. She took two quick bites and then threw the spoon at Errol.

"What was that for?" he asked, barely dodging the flying spoon.

"Who in their right mind tries to bribe a preacher?"

Errol looked like a kid caught with his hand in the cookie jar.

"Oh, he told you about that?"

"You bet your sweet ass, he did, and guess what?"

"What?"

"You're still buying the church a bus," Clarke replied. "I go to church there, Errol, and I won't have the pastor looking at me funny because of some old crazy shit you said. Who does that, huh? Errol, who tries to bribe a pastor?"

"You got me. Just let it go, Clarke. We'll buy the damned bus." Errol smiled.

Suddenly, Clarke wasn't so mad anymore. She

couldn't blame Errol for trying. If the truth be told, she didn't want to go either.

Clarke batted her eyes at her man. He was no stranger to the gesture. "What do you want now, babe?"

"I need another spoon, please," Clarke replied, embarrassed.

"Too bad, so sad." Errol laughed. "You shouldn't have hurled that one at me."

You Gotta Talk to Somebody

Dee moved the wire whisk back and forth in the bowl filled with eggs. It had only been a week, and Hiram had her all the way open. They'd been inseparable since last Sunday's dinner. Hiram followed her home to chat over a cup of coffee, and the rest was history.

Talking to Hiram was so easy. Dee was comfortable with him. She could be herself completely. She didn't have to hide behind semantics with him. She could keep it completely real.

Dee smiled as Hiram came up behind her. He wrapped his arms around her waist and planted a kiss on the nape of her neck. She poured the frothing liquid into the pan and swatted him away, stirring the eggs with one spatula and grabbing another whisk to stir the grits. She'd become quite the housewife over the last week, and it felt great. Suddenly, Dee had someone to come home to every day, and they both seemed to enjoy it.

Dee opened the microwave door, inserted the bacon tray, hit the number four, and slid the eggs onto their serving tray in one fluid movement. She stirred the grits again, gave Hiram a quick peck, and went to throw a load of clothes into the washer.

Dee grabbed a pile of sorted clothes and carried them to the laundry room. She turned on the water, added the detergent, and began to turn Hiram's $700 Dolce and Gabbana jeans inside out when a small white rectangle hit the floor. She bent over to pick up the same card she had in her own bag.

Dee stopped dead in her tracks as she looked as the card in her hand. What in the hell was Hiram up to? She turned to march back to the kitchen, only to find Hiram standing there smiling as she loaded the washer. As he watched Dee's reaction to her unexpected find, the smile suddenly disappeared from his face. He saw Dee as she read Officer Rouche's card for the second time.

She turned to him, holding the card up in the air. "Are you working with a cop?"

"Dee, it's not what you think."

"What exactly am I thinking?" Dee asked.

"You're thinking that I'm a snitch. You're thinking that I've turned, and I can't be trusted," Hiram replied.

"I am not sure what to think, Hiram."

"It's really complicated," Hiram replied.

"Why don't you make it simple for me?" Dee demanded.

"I don't expect you to understand, but do you know what it feels like to be next in line, knowing you will never rule? Do you know how it feels to do someone's dirty work and never be appreciated?"

Dee could completely relate, but she refused to nod her head just yet.

"I know it's only been a week, but I want to be with you for the long haul. I don't have to hide who I am, what I do, or the real me. You get me. You understand me, and right now I need you to understand this," Hiram pleaded.

"Understand what?" Dee inquired.

"I wasn't exactly happy with my career choice or my position within our company. Then one day, Vincent approached me and promised to give me the Port City to run if I would give him the information he needed to get Errol and Clarke off the street. He really has it in for them. I ain't no snitch, but what's wrong with wanting my place at the top? I'm tired of being their errand boy. I'm tired of being the one to get my hands dirty for peanuts. I want it all."

Dee let out a sigh of relief. "What are the chances of the same officer approaching me?"

"I already know, Dee. I was in the car the night he pulled you over for drinking and swerving," Hiram replied.

"So you've known this all the time?" Dee asked.

"Why do you think I lingered around when you stayed in that bathroom so long, or why I tried to come check on you after you passed out? I was afraid they'd found you out and would try to harm you."

Tears filled Dee's eyes. It had been so long since she felt that someone actually had her back. The card fell from her hand as she walked over to embrace her man. Tears of joy ran down her face as she realized that she wouldn't be squaring off with Dee, Errol, and the Kings alone.

"Is it safe to say that you won't be ratting me out, Dee?" Hiram asked.

"You bet your ass it's safe." Dee replied as she wiped a tear running down her face. "I have a partner in the bedroom and out here in these streets. A girl like me couldn't ask for more."

"Are you ready to take your place by my side as the head of the Kings?" Hiram questioned.

"Absolutely! I've had a secret desire to shake things up for a while now. Especially since my last boyfriend went to a meeting with Clarke and never came home. Nobody will tell me what happened, but I know she killed him. I've just been biding my time," Dee said as she stared off into space.

Hiram extended his right hand, "So, let's take them down together."

"You got it, Hiram. You got it," Dee said as she and her new partner shook hands. Then they returned to the kitchen to enjoy their first breakfast as cohorts.

***

Errol held a cold towel on Clarke's head as she blew chunks into the toilet. Her morning sickness was getting worse. Ginger ale and crackers weren't enough to prevent the nausea anymore. He handed her another cloth for her mouth once she straightened up.

"Babe, we can call Reverend Dubois and cancel if you're not feeling well," Errol suggested.

"Not a chance, babe. We are gonna be there, happy to write that $100,000 check."

Errol grimaced as he opened the door for Anna to bring in breakfast: oatmeal, a banana, and bacon for Errol, and apple slices, peanut butter, and grapes for Clarke.

Clarke met Errol in the sitting room. He placed her plate on the table beside her and had a seat in the chair on the opposite side of the room.

"Are you ready for the questions this man may ask?" Errol queried, smacking on a piece of bacon.

"You bet. We're not going to talk about work, babe. Stop worrying. He's only going to ask about our relationship and our problem-solving skills. Do we communicate, or don't we? Do we know how to kiss and make up, or do we let things linger? You are really making this deeper than it is. Today is about us, not what we do."

"Do you know how much I love you?" Errol asked.

"I have an idea," Clarke responded flirtatiously.

"Well, love, are you ready to go pour out our hearts? We wouldn't want to be late." Errol said now that he was feeling more confident about today's meeting.

"I'm ready when you are," Clarke responded.

Errol crossed the room to help his fiancée to her feet, down the stairs, and into the car.

***

While Clarke and Errol were on their way to meet Reverend Dubois, Dee and Hiram were in a meeting of their own.

"Are you two sure you have the stomach for this?" Vincent Rouche inquired.

Dee and Hiram sat holding hands. Hiram replied, "Yep. We're ready to get them out of the way and put ourselves in a position to get more of this money."

"That's fine, as long as you mean *our* money," Vincent replied.

"Of course," Hiram said. "We'll definitely make sure you get your third."

"That's good to hear, Hiram," Vincent responded.

However, Dee wasn't as convincing. She'd been quiet during the bulk of their meeting.

"Dee, are you okay?" Vincent asked. "You've been mighty quiet."

"I was processing all this information. Keep in mind, you just gave us the instructions to send our friends to the slammer while we take their positions. It's a lot to take in at once," Dee explained.

"Do you have any questions, Dee? Are your instructions straightforward enough?"

"Oh, yeah, yeah. I just can't stop thinking about what could have been," Dee responded.

"Too late for that. Now we have to focus on what is," Vincent said as he stood up.

"Your sit-down is on Friday night before the wedding, and the deal is the next day. You guys just be ready. We only have four days," Vincent said. He placed his hat on his head and closed the door behind him.

***

Clarke had never seen Errol as nervous as he was on

their way to Bennettsville Missionary Baptist Church.

"Baby, why are you so uneasy?" Clarke probed.

"I don't often put myself in positions that require me to answer someone's questions. It's just bad for business," Errol said.

"Why do you assume these questions will relate to work? They won't. They're all about us a couple."

"That's what scares me."

"I don't get it." Clarke was growing annoyed. "You're really putting too much into this. Why don't you believe me when I say it's really not that deep?"

"You've never been to marriage counseling before, so how do you know? Let's hope you're right. Now, no more questions. Let's just enjoy the drive."

Errol placed his hand over Clarke's on the armrest and gave it a soft squeeze. He looked over to her and smiled, searching her face for a glimpse of understanding.

Clarke returned his smile and gave an empathetic nod. Suddenly the tension flew right out of the sunroof. The rest of the ride was enjoyable as the sun fell through the open roof onto them both.

Errol finally pulled into a massive parking lot and parked on the first row next to the pastor's assigned space. It was empty and for a moment, Errol was a bit relieved.

"Well, he's not here. We can go now," Errol remarked to Clarke.

"I'm sure he's just a minute or two behind, babe. Let's go in and speak with Ms. Holland, the secretary," Clarke replied.

Errol grimaced like a child refusing his vegetables. "Okay, Clarke. This is just for you. Today is all because I love you."

"I know, my heart," Clarke said. She leaned over and kissed Errol on the cheek.

He finally released her hand and powered off the car. He was walking around it to open Clarke's door as Reverend Dubois drove up.

He jumped from his Ford Expedition and walked over to the couple as Errol helped Clarke from the car.

"I'm so glad you two could make it," Reverend Dubois began. "I know you guys may have been a little anxious about counseling, but it will be painless. I promise," the pastor said.

"Good thing, sir. I am no fan of counseling," Errol said.

Clarke quickly nudged him in the ribcage with her elbow.

Reverend Dubois laughed and held the door open for the couple as they entered the vestibule of the church. "Good morning, Ms. Holland," Reverend Dubois said as he peeked his head into the open door off to the left side of the massive foyer. She politely responded and handed him two folders, one blue and the other pink.

Reverend Dubois spoke to the couple from the other side of the room. "Please, follow me this way to my office."

Errol and Clarke, now holding hands, followed the pastor down a fairly long corridor to a small corner office. It had a big window overlooking Greenfield Lake, its joggers, the kids in the park, and the city's newest love stories. He had little space, but he was able to see life and its different perspectives from here, and that suited him just fine.

"Have a seat, and please make yourself comfortable," Reverend Dubois said as he pointed to the two wingback chairs that sat facing each other and the desk. Errol helped Clarke into the chair on the left, and he settled into the one on the right.

Reverend Dubois set humbly behind a small oak desk covered with files and yellow sticky notes. His leather chair had a small crack in the headrest, but somehow it fit the office perfectly.

The pastor immediately placed his head in the cracked spot. Then he rolled the chair up closer to his desk and the couple, stretched out both his arms, and said, "Let's join hands in prayer before we begin."

Errol looked over at Clarke, a bit unnerved by the situation, but he quickly followed suit.

Reverend Dubois began to pray, "Dear Father God, we come humbly before you, thanking you for life, health, and strength. We honor you and pray that you give us words today. We pray that everything said and done is pleasing in your sight, and we count it done. In Jesus's name we pray. Amen."

"Thank you both for coming in to speak with me today," Reverend Dubois continued. "I know you both are very busy."

"No, thank you for agreeing to preside over our nuptials on such short notice," Errol said.

"I am always glad to bring two people together—when it's right, that is," Reverend Dubois replied.

"What do you mean, if it's right? Who are you to decide?" Errol countered, looking annoyed.

Clarke leaned to the right and put her head in her hand. Errol glanced her way, and Clarke began to speak. "How do you determine who's right for whom? Do you have a test?"

"Actually, I do, but let's consider this; If you have two people before you who don't agree on how to work through life's stresses, such as how to pay bills, how to discipline their children, how to overcome obstacles from within your home, and especially those who come from without—would you consider them a couple who should be together?"

"I think a woman should submit to the wishes of her husband. I think it should be a thing that becomes second nature to a wife," Errol said.

"Clarke, how do you feel about that?" the pastor questioned.

"I have no problem submitting to my husband," Clarke said.

Reverend Dubois raised his eyebrows and listened

intently.

Clarke continued. "I watched my grandparents when I was small, and I always knew that was the type of marriage I wanted with my husband. I wanted the old-school marriage. So I don't have a problem following or taking direction from the man I believe God put in my life—as strange as that may sound. Does that sound strange to you, Pastor Dubois?" Clarke queried.

"Errol, how does that make you feel?" The pastor turned to face Errol now.

"I am humbled. This is something she's always told me, and I make it my business to try and live up to those expectations daily. I know that she trusts me to make the hard decisions for our family, and I know that she'll always do her best to advise me properly. I am blessed to be with such a woman."

"Wow, you two definitely have the right foundation. Many marriages fail because they don't have this type of understanding, and it sometimes leads to chaos. You said the hard decisions, Errol. Give me an example of a hard decision you've had to make recently."

Errol looked questioningly over to Clarke. She smiled.

Then he began, "Clarke wants me to leave a business that has been extremely profitable for my family because of its stresses and risks, and she's probably right. I just can't do it right now."

"How do you feel about that, Clarke?" the pastor asked.

"I love him so much, and I don't want to see myself without him. I understand the importance of what he does and what his leadership means to his family, but I want my husband to come home happy and safe every night, not stressed and worried about how something or someone else could impact business or our family."

"I get that, babe, but I need you to stand by me until the day comes that I can walk away," Errol pleaded.

"I'll agree on one condition," Clarke offered.

"Anything."

"Please promise me you'll at least take a step back and work on your stress level."

"You got it!" Errol promised. He leaned over and kissed Clarke on the cheek.

Reverend Dubois smiled as he looked at a couple lost

in love. "You guys are gonna be fine," he said. "Let's get through this questionnaire now."

For the next hour, Errol, Clarke, and Reverend Dubois exchanged laughs. He was impressed that they recognized each other's triggers and had great communication and the same beliefs on child rearing and homemaking.

"Thank you for coming in today," Reverend Dubois said as he wrapped things up.

"Thank you for having us," Errol responded as he reached in his pocket and pulled out a piece of paper. He handed the pastor a $100,000 check for the new church bus.

Reverend Dubois thanked the couple again and again, hugged their necks, and called in the church secretary. She was just as amazed and grateful.

"We were glad to be able to sew a seed here in this great place. Thank you for allowing us to be a part of such a great spiritual family. So, Rev? Did we pass? Can we get married?"

"Absolutely, you guys are perfect for each other. Clarke, just do your best to keep this gentleman out of trouble. Errol, make sure you both take your problems to God, and know that he is never too far away to hear your call. He can save you!"

"Thank you for your time, Pastor," Errol said. He quickly reached for Clarke's hand, and they were off to another meeting.

***

Errol and Clarke visited the Marley Grill for the first time as a couple since his release. Clarke didn't like going there anymore. She wanted nothing more than to distance herself from the entire situation. She only agreed today because of her love for Errol and because she had a plan to rid them of the Kings for good.

Errol led Clarke to the kitchen with his hand on the small of her back. The cousins all nodded hello as they passed the domino table.

Clarke remembered the days when she came in the grill wanting to know more about this tall, dark, and strange man. Things were so simple then. His "cousins" were just well-dressed bums then. Now she knew that each man at that table was a trained killer hiding behind a gold chain and a smile.

They opened the kitchen door and walked to the back office with the funny-looking ceiling. There were three men sitting on one side of the table and two on the other with an empty seat closest to the head of the table for Clarke.

Errol helped her into her seat and then took his own at the head of the table.

Admiral began to speak. "Everything is all set now. We have a new skeleton crew. These guys are fresh off the boat and willing to do anything we ask. They're not afraid of a bit of jail time. At any rate, it's better than the infighting they faced in Haiti. They are meeting Mafietta and the King for the first time on Friday night, and the deal will go down on Saturday."

"Saturday!? What about the wedding? I will not have my wedding day ruined," Clarke argued.

Errol placed a hand on her thigh, and Clarke let that be the conclusion of her argument.

"Don't worry, lil' sis. This will all be over by two. You two aren't getting married until six. You'll be fine. I guarantee it," Admiral promised.

"You'd better be right," Clarke snapped as she grabbed her bag and stood to her feet. "Are we done here?"

"Yep, we're done," Admiral said curtly.

"We thought you'd left Mafietta at home, but we see she's back," Lil' Stupid joked. The room roared with laughter as the couple exited the room, attempting to hide their own amusement.

***

"I don't want to be her anymore," Clarke confessed.

"Be who?" Errol asked.

"I don't want to be Mafietta anymore. I want to go back to the days when I was blind to the things you do. I want to be innocent again. Can you promise me that? I can work with God on the rest, just promise me that."

Errol took one hand from the wheel and wiped the tears from Clarke's face.

"I promise, babe," he replied with teary eyes.

"No more blood?" Clarke asked.

"No, babe. No more blood."

"I have one more request." Clarke informed Errol while blowing her nose.

"What's that, my love?" he asked.

"Your baby wants Bojangles fries and cake batter ice cream from Maggy Moo." Clarke smiled.

Errol looked suspiciously over to Clarke. "Are you sure my little one wants all of this?"

They both smiled, and Clarke said, "Yep!"

"Anything for my babies," Errol joked as he made a U-turn at the light to head to Maggy Moo.

The Last Supper

Word of Mafietta and the King spread like wildfire across the water to Haiti, from a little gunboat to the big man of the island. He was very interested in doing business with the Kings. He didn't mind sacrificing a few members of his clan to establish a strong relationship with them either. Should our deal go south, they would most likely be deported back to Haiti, where they would have enough money to live like kings themselves.

Toussaint, Leandre, and Nikolas could do very little to hide their accents as they spoke with Mafietta and the King at the Marley Grill. Hiram and the men exchanged pleasantries in French. Dee listened attentively. She had no idea what they were saying, but the flow of the words sounded nice.

Dee was there as a display piece, and this annoyed her at first, but once they began to pass around a humongous spliff, she didn't mind at all. It allowed her a moment to enjoy her high without keeping up with the bullshit conversation she was forced to endure.

After a few tokes of some pretty strong stuff, Dee

said, "All right, guys, enough with that French shit. I have no idea what you are saying—English, please!"

The men looked baffled, but for only a second. They'd heard stories of Mafietta's wrath.

"Whatever you say, Mafietta. We've heard stories about you and have nothing but respect," Toussaint replied.

"Stories? What exactly have you heard about me?"

"We heard about the time you had Black shaking in his shoes for disrespecting you," Leandre said.

"And we heard about how you made an entire group of men open legitimate businesses," Toussaint added.

"We also heard about that time you shot that dude in a meeting for talking shit after the King got knocked. You are gangsta. Did they ever find that body?" Nikolas said.

A ton of bricks hit Dee in her chest and all of the air escaped her body. She couldn't move, and she couldn't take her next breath. She didn't have the strength. She gasped for breath as she regained consciousness.

She was slumped down in the booth's corner seat as air began to fill her body again. Her heart was breaking, and she was enraged, but couldn't show it. The next hour was hell for Dee. She smiled, nodded, and laughed when necessary, despite the fact that she felt complete emptiness and rage.

The couple showed their new Haitian friends to the door, and then Dee collapsed onto the bar's first stool. Hiram rushed over to her and asked, "Are you okay? What can I do?"

"I knew it. I knew it. I can't wait until tomorrow when I can be done with this trifling bitch once and for all."

Dee was one meeting away from crushing her nemesis.

***

Hiram and Dee missed the rehearsal, the dinner, and the party that followed, but Errol and Clarke didn't care. Their absence was one less reminder of the impending tribulations. The church was partially decorated, and it was beautiful.

Each window was decorated with arrangements of pink, purple, and white flowers. Midsize chandeliers were installed all over the sanctuary, which was covered with silk curtains and sashes. The choir loft was no longer visible. That area was completely covered by greenery and fresh pink and purple flowers. A silver candelabra stood in front of the floral collage. The pulpit was empty, and there was still much to do, but it was a beautiful sight as it was.

Clarke forced Errol to the church to take a final look before their wedding. When they got there, the room was dark, and only the kneeling bench in the center of the pulpit, illuminated by a spotlight, could be seen.

Clarke grabbed Errol's hand and began to march down the aisle toward the altar. The couple could barely see their feet in front of them, but Clarke didn't let that stop her.

As they came closer to the kneeling bench, the path became clear. Clarke hurried her pace but held on to Errol's hand—forcing him to do the same. She jogged up the stairs leading to the bench and fell to her knees. Errol walked around curiously and knelt on the opposite side to face his wife to be.

He knelt there, powerless against her tears. He held her hands as puddles of tears spilled onto the silk covering the armrest of the kneeling bench. Errol stroked her hair as her body began to convulse, and the tears came more heavily, robbing her of her breath.

Errol jumped to his feet and knelt behind the desire of his heart. He held her until her body became still.

"Are you okay, babe?" Errol asked, unable to hide his concern.

"I'm feeling great now. I left it all here. All the blood, all the lies, all of the past—I left it here," Clarke said as she smiled through tears.

Errol wiped her face, kissed her forehead, and helped her to her feet. He hugged his fiancée with a fierceness that sent shockwaves pulsing through Clarke's body. She knew he loved her. She could feel it.

"Baby, I really don't feel like going out. I'm fine with just going home," Clarke said to Errol.

"You know what, I don't either. Let's go home together," Errol offered.

"Are you sure you want to miss your bachelor party, babe?"

"Yep, I'm sure. I'd rather throw my bills at you anyway," Errol joked.

"Come on, man. Let's get out of here," Clarke said as she led Errol toward the exit at the rear of the room.

Clarke was winded by the time they reached the door. She placed her hands on the wall to steady herself and suddenly the room was filled with light. She and Errol stood in awe of Eliza-Beth's work. Clarke leaned into Errol, and he wrapped his arms around her. They enjoyed the peace and beauty of the moment. Clarke decided to leave the light on, and the couple turned to go home.

The First Day of Forever

Eliza-Beth could not understand why Clarke wanted to wait so late in the day to have her makeup done. They'd just made the final walk-through at the church, and everything was even more beautiful than last night. Flowers filled the room like wallpaper. They were beginning to fill the sanctuary with a wonderful floral scent. Each pew was decorated with a flower arrangement, and the pulpit was covered with pink rose petals. It was an amazing sight, definitely worthy of inclusion in any bridal magazine.

Eliza-Beth mentioned having the photos submitted to *Carolina Bride*, but Clarke was a million miles away. Her thoughts were of tying up the mess named Dee.

"Clarke, what do you think?" Eliza-Beth asked.

"Liza, I'm sorry," Clarke said, snapping back to reality. "I missed that. What did you say?"

"Is there no way you can make it to hair and makeup before three o'clock? You are really giving my glam squad a run for their money," Eliza-Beth said.

"I don't mind as long as I am beautiful," Clarke joked.

Eliza-Beth frowned.

Clarke continued, "I'm sorry. Errol and I have had this thing planned for months. I couldn't get away." Clarke looked at her watch. She had thirty minutes left to get to Errol to finalize this deal.

***

"I hate to put such pressure on you at the last minute, dude, but I just can't make it today. I wanted to do this myself, but I am sure you can handle things. I've even made it worth your while," the figure said as he tossed two small stacks of hundreds still in the $2,000 band.

"No worries, man. This will work just fine," the other figure replied.

"What time is your 'Mafietta,' as our Haitian connection calls her, gonna meet you?" the leader inquired.

"I am going to pick up the car at twelve thirty, and she'll meet me at the spot. Then we'll drive over together to handle things for you. That's what's up."

The leader said, "We gotta get that paper, man. Are you sure you have this covered?"

"You bet your ass, I do. I've been waiting for a chance to prove myself, and I really want to thank you for this opportunity. And who knows, I may be better at this than you."

The hidden figure let out a small throaty laugh. "I'm counting on it."

***

Clarke met Errol in another back room of the Marley Grill just moments before the deal was due to begin. Errol was sitting in the corner of the room on a leather sectional. He smiled as he watched Clarke waddle over to him. He helped her down into the seat and asked, "Are you ready for this ride?"

"I'm as ready as I'll ever be. If is the path to clean hands and no more blood, I'm all for it," Clarke replied. "We have a great day ahead of us. Let's just get this over with."

Errol's phone rang. "Yeah, man. Gotcha. We're on it."

He reached to the table for a small remote. He pressed the green button and the sixty-inch flat screen came to life.

Each quadrant of the television displayed a different location. The first one showed the inside of a black Mercedes E-500. The couple watched as the car came to a stop, and the driver picked up a passenger.

"Are you ready for this?" the man asked the woman.

"Hell, yeah. I am ready to see this bitch burn."

Clarke squirmed in her seat on the couch as a feeling of uneasiness began to swallow her whole.

"She really hates me, Errol," Clarke said, looking to Errol for support.

"No one gives a damn how she feels. She dug this mudhole. Now she can wallow in it," Errol said.

Clarke looked over to him and saw a face she'd only seen once. Errol's eyes weren't soft and caring anymore. They were hard and fierce. She wasn't looking into the face of her loving fiancé and father to be. She looked at her man, and for the first time, she saw the face of a killer.

She looked up to the screen. The couple continued to speak.

"Dee, are you ready to bring Clarke and Errol to their knees?" Hiram asked.

"You damned right. Do you know what it felt like to finally know that Clarke killed my Mike? I've worked with and for this woman, picked out her clothes, done her hair, made her drops, and picked up her cash—and she killed my man! She deserves everything we have coming her way."

"It's about time someone knocked these Kings right off their throne," Hiram agreed. "They parade around here hiding behind businesses and accountants, but they are no better than me. I can run this thing better than them all, especially Errol. It's time for Errol to get off the throne and out of my damned way."

Errol growled at the screen. Clarke could see him becoming more and more enraged by the moment. She looked at him, uneasy as she faced the man she didn't recognize.

Errol pointed at the screen and said, "It's happening. Look!"

Dee and Hiram walked into a small room in the back of Wendy's Salon and Hair Gallery. Their view faded from the car's internal camera, but returned within seconds on the second quadrant of the screen. The couple each took a key and unlocked two floor safes full of powder cocaine.

Dee walked over to a cabinet and pulled out a bottle of Hennessey, two glasses, and a spliff. "Be prepared," she said to Hiram jokingly as she poured him a drink.

Hiram held up his glass to propose a toast. "Here's to severing old ties and making more money. Cheers!"

"Cheers!" Dee threw back her double shot. She lit the blunt, puffed it, and passed it to Hiram. She was pouring herself another drink as Hiram announced that their guests had arrived.

He opened the door to Toussaint, Leandre, and Nikolas.

"Greetings, gentlemen," Dee said as she showed the men to their seats across the room.

"Good afternoon, Mafietta," Toussaint responded.

Dee laughed but said, "Good afternoon."

Hiram didn't believe in spending a lot of time doing this type of thing, so he was clearly ready to wrap things up. "Do you have the cash?"

"The trunk is full of it," Nikolas said.

"The trunk may be full, but is that all of it?" Hiram queried.

"Of course, my friend. We look forward to a long working relationship with you." Toussaint said.

"There are ten bricks in each cabinet," Dee advised. "All twenty are yours."

"Sorry we can't stay to help you pack, but we have a wedding to crash," Hiram added.

He tossed a set of keys over to Nikolas. "Take the black Benz, and bring it back here once you've unloaded it."

"No worries," Toussiant replied happily.

"Hate to run, but we have another appointment," Dee explained as she held out her hand.

Toussaint handed her keys to the money-green Camaro waiting outside.

"Thank you, gentlemen. It's been a pleasure," Dee said. Hiram held the door and exited behind her.

Their Haitian connection was left alone to move their own product. However, instead of taking the drugs, they closed each of the safes, and Nikolas pulled a burner phone from his pocket.

Errol watched from a camera perched on the rear corner wall of the salon's exterior. Hiram popped open the trunk lined with two hundred grand, just as his friends promised. He removed twenty thousand dollars and quickly tossed Dee half. He closed the truck and entered the car.

"Damn!" Errol banged his hands on the table. "Does everyone steal from me?"

Clarke sat quietly, watching the screen, but also observing a man she loved but didn't recognize.

Dee and Hiram now filled the third quadrant of the television screen as they sat in the Camaro's brown, butter-soft bucket seats. "We have to hurry," Dee advised Hiram. "I promised Clarke that I'd meet her at two. What Clarke doesn't know is that I'm coming with the drop that will send Mafietta and her King away for a long time."

Hiram shouted, "Woo-hoo! We did it. We actually did it. Once we give them this money, they're history."

"Did you bring the two kilos from the vault?" Dee asked.

"Hell, yeah!" Hiram responded. "What will the cops think when they find two kilos and two hundred grand in the happy couple's brand new ride?"

"They'll think they hit the mother lode, and we can keep getting this money," Dee responded.

Hiram took the bricks and placed them in the enlarged glove compartment of the Camaro. "Fuck Errol Bellow and the Port City Kings. We takin' over!"

Errol fumed as he watched the disrespect the two flung around. He'd had enough. He reached to pick up his phone.

Errol punched numbers into the phone and within seconds screamed, "I've had enough. Get those snitching bitches now!" Clarke heard glass shatter as Errol slammed the phone onto the table. She sat, almost afraid to move. She didn't know the figure sitting before her. Suddenly, she questioned everything.

She didn't have much time to consider her thoughts because moments later, flashing blue lights pulled up behind Hiram and Dee.

"That's probably Officer Rouche coming to check on us," Dee said in response to the lights in their rearview mirror. The couple remained calm and began to pull to the side of the road when they noticed another car approaching.

This one cut them off. Two officers jumped out.

"What the hell is going on?" Dee demanded.

"You tell me," Hiram shouted.

Errol laughed aloud as he watched the two bicker. Clarke looked back and forth between Errol and the screen. The entire situation left her speechless.

"I don't give a fuck. I have nothing to lose," Dee said. "I don't care if I go down, but that bitch and her kingpin husband are going down, too."

She rolled down the window and stuck out both her hands.

Errol and Clarke watched as the officers handcuffed the couple and began to search the car.

"You have no right to search our car," Hiram insisted.

"We had a call that someone in a green Camaro was selling drugs on College Road. We're just checking it out."

"Oh, shit," an officer exclaimed as he examined the trunk. "This thing is full of money."

Another officer opened the glove box and found the cocaine. "Dang, Bonnie and Clyde!" the officer remarked. "I think it's time we read you your rights."

Neither Hiram nor Dee offered the cops any information. Dee only spoke once. "Officer Smith," she said, reading his badge, "Would you please call Detective Rouche? He can explain."

"Is this some kind of trick?" the officer asked.

"What do you mean, trick?" Hiram retorted. "We've been working with him for weeks."

"I'm sorry, guys. We don't have anyone by that name on our force."

Dee placed her head into her handcuffed hands. The joke was on her.

***

Clarke looked over as Errol watched Hiram and Dee be dragged away. She expected a look of relief, but instead she saw consternation.

He slowly picked up the phone and made a second call. "Finish them," he whispered.

Clarke looked over at Errol in amazement. Then to the screen.

Suddenly the screen was filled with flames as car parts shot up into the air.

"What have you done?" Clarke screamed. "What the fuck did you just do?" Tears fell down her face by the bucket. "You promised me there wouldn't be any more blood on my hands, Errol. You promised."

She looked at him and was overtaken with rage. She pummeled him with fist after fist as she screamed, "How can you live with yourself? You are a killer. You do this shit all the time. I can't be with you. My child can't know you. Call off the wedding, Errol."

She picked up the phone and threw it at his chest. "Call it *off*!" she shrieked. "I don't want you, and my child won't know you. You're dead to me."

Errol was on his feet within seconds. He grabbed Clarke by the arms and looked her in the eyes. "You don't mean that, Clarke. You know we had to do that to make sure they didn't talk," Errol said unconvincingly.

"Fuck you, and fuck this," Clarke screamed through tears and clenched teeth. "The wedding is off. I'm getting as far away from you and this shit as gas allows."

This only enraged Errol even more. Suddenly, Clarke was face to face with a man she'd never met but was due to marry. His eyes were filled with hatred, and the hands that wrapped around her arms began to shake her. First slowly and then more viciously.

"Clarke, you can't leave me, and you damn sure ain't taking my baby," Errol shouted, inches away from Clarke's face.

"I'm gone, and you can't stop me," Clarke retorted.

Suddenly a hand came from the sky, and pain filled one side of Clarke's face. She lifted her hand to return the blow, but Errol grabbed it and pushed her to the couch.

He held her down and bellowed, "You can't leave me. This is forever, and if you try, I will carve my child out of you and throw your body in the fucking Atlantic Ocean."

"You punk! How dare you threaten me? Have you forgotten who I am? I am Mafietta!"

Errol released his fiancée and remarked, "My point exactly. You are no better than me. We are who we are, and you and I are a couple. You'd better get that registered pretty quickly, love. We have a wedding in about three hours."

"I'm not going to show up, Errol. You are wasting your time. You promised me you'd stop killing people. I can't go through with this. What about your son? Don't you want a better life for him?"

Errol veered at Clarke, leaned in, and forced his tongue into her mouth. She tried to fight him, but he was too strong, and she dared not harm her unborn child.

Errol stood and wiped his mouth on the sleeve of his shirt. "Don't you have a hair appointment you should be getting to? Oh, and you should tell your grandmother you won't be needing that apartment."

With that, Errol turned and left Clarke there wallowing in her mountain of tears and regret.

***

"Girl, it's about time you got here. We have less than an hour to do your hair and makeup, and get you dressed," Eliza-Beth said as she moved around nervously.

"Sorry, Liza. I had some business that wouldn't wait."

"It's all water under the bridge now," Eliza-Beth said as she patted Clarke on the leg. "Marcy, get something for these puffy eyes."

Clarke was surprised to find a box waiting for her when she arrived. She opened it as Liza's glam squad began to work its magic. The small box held a set of baby keys and a note that said, "You still hold the keys to my heart. This is forever."

Her head was spinning. How could she marry a monster like Errol? How long would it be before she did something to piss him off and found herself on the other side of his wrath? She would have to figure something out, but for now there had to be a wedding. She turned on the television to clear her thoughts.

She was laughing at Kevin Hart's commercial for his newest movies when WECT came on with breaking news. "The couple known to the underworld as 'Mafietta and the King' is now dead. They were victims of an explosion after being taken into police custody. Port City police are now investigating the cause of the blow up. More to come at six."

Clarke had to admit that this was a smart move, even though the thought of more death sent her reeling. She tossed the keys onto the table next to her bouquet. Then her thoughts were interrupted by a knock at the door.

She heard the room quiet as Eliza-Beth told Errol,

"Mr. Bellow, it is bad luck to see your bride before the wedding."

"I don't believe in luck, Ms. Rushing. Tell Clarke I need to speak to her."

"It's okay," Clarke said.

"Um, we don't have much time left, Clarke. You're going to be cutting it close," Eliza-Beth said.

"This will only take a second. All I have left now is to step into my dress. We'll be fine. Clear the room, ladies," Clarke ordered.

Within seconds, the room was empty and quiet.

Clarke reached for her purse as Errol entered.

"Are we all set, love?" Errol asked.

"You just threatened my life, and now you ask if we're all set?"

"The show must go on, Clarke. I love you. Don't let business get in the way of that," Errol pleaded. "I won't live without you."

Clarke summoned the strength that fueled her actions while Errol was away and stood to her feet, squaring off with her man. She pulled a baby 380 from her purse and placed it on Errol's temple. He didn't blink.

"I am Mafietta, and if you ever threaten me again, you won't have to worry about coming for me. I'm gonna drop your ass right then and there."

Errol laughed as he wrapped his arms around the love of his life. "I don't want to lose you. This thing between us works. No one else could do this."

"Maybe you should remember that." Clarke responded jokingly. "Now help me into my dress. I have a King to marry."

ABOUT THE AUTHOR

"I hope to continue to put out content that people want to read. If something I write can take someone away from the stresses of their day, I've accomplished my goal. I don't seek to change the world with my books—I have a blog for that—but I do hope to entertain it."
—E. W. Brooks

Growing up in a small town fueled E. W.'s desire to see more and led her to larger cities where she always kept abreast of events via the nightly news and local newspapers. Brooks was intrigued by the stories of those who made an effort at a better life on the wrong side of the law. Her curiosities led to much research and her writing of *Mafietta*.

E. W. Brooks is an army wife, big sister, and mentor with a big imagination. She is the founder of the Campbell Sisterhood, a group of women who support and empower each other as well as other army wives. Brooks also donates 10 percent of book proceeds to the Military Matters Project. However, she says, her greatest joys come from spending time with her family and seeing the smiling faces of those she's helped to find a bit of light along their journey.

Printed in Great Britain
by Amazon